Joanna cradled Karen's breast as firelight danced in golden shadows across her tawny skin.

Joanna bent forward over Karen's full breasts. Karen gasped as Joanna took her nipple into her mouth, covering it completely with her tongue. Shocks of excitement surged through her. Passion moved through her veins like liquid light. She undressed Karen hungrily, then slid her hand along her inner thigh.

More than anything in the world, she wanted to fill Karen with pleasure.

Her fingers moved in the hot wet silk, separating Karen's lips, circling the firmness of the pearl, moving slowly again along the silky lips, sliding slowly inside . . .

About the Author

Evelyn Kennedy brings a varied background to the art of fiction. She spent several years as a cloistered nun, completed a tour of duty as a paramedic with the military, taught on the University and Nursing School levels, holds a brown belt in Karate, writes poetry for her own enjoyment, and admits to being an incurable romantic. Her first novel *Cherished Love*, and her second novel, *Of Love and Glory*, were best sellers.

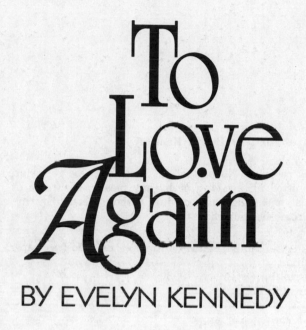

To Love Again

BY EVELYN KENNEDY

The Naiad Press, Inc.
1997

Copyright © 1991 by Evelyn Kennedy

Printed in the United States of America on acid-free paper
First Edition
Second Printing December, 1993
Third Printing February, 1997

Edited by Christine Cassidy
Cover design by Pat Tong and Bonnie Liss
     (Phoenix Graphics)
Typeset by Sandi Stancil

Library of Congress Cataloging-in-Publication Data

Kennedy, Evelyn, 1939 /–
    To love again / by Evelyn Kennedy.
        p.   cm.
    ISBN 0-941483-85-1
    I. Title.
PS3561.E4263T6   1991
813'.54—dc20   91-25253
                                                          CIP

For all women who have spent
too many hours in closets

CHAPTER 1

Karen Wainwright glanced in her rearview mirror just in time to see a flashing blue light — an Atlanta police car pulled around a dark green pick-up truck and sped in her direction. Sirens seemed to come out of nowhere, but the speedometer read thirty-five. "I'm not speeding," she said aloud, breathing a sigh of relief. She certainly didn't need a third speeding ticket to explain to Phillip. She steered to the far right of Ponce de Leon Avenue and slowed down. The siren screamed past her and the flashing blue light disappeared several blocks ahead. As she eased into the main line of traffic, another flashing blue light and high-pitched siren materialized at her left. She pulled the car sharply to the right. "Idiot!" she shouted at the red-headed police officer behind the wheel. Her heart thumped against her chest. They were probably after some poor slob who went through a yellow light, she thought. If only they were that dedicated to catching drug dealers.

The parking lot was exactly where the receptionist had said it would be, and she could feel her pulse return to normal as she locked the car and walked toward the women's clinic. She had always hated the first day on a new job, and today was no exception, but she still hadn't expected the anxiety. After all, she thought, it's not like it's a regular job. Being a volunteer would allow her the freedom she needed. She smiled as she realized that she sounded just like the volunteers who had driven her crazy at Saint Joseph's. Phillip would love that.

Atlanta's side streets and major thoroughfares were lined with trees and shrubbery. Two large magnolia trees, their branches filled with big white flowers, perfumed the air with a sweetness known only in the South. Rows of pink, white and red azaleas bordered the front yards of almost every house she passed. Here and there, tall oleander bushes, heavy with deep lavender-pink blossoms, added their unique beauty to Atlanta's spring explosion.

There wasn't a more beautiful city in the world, Karen mused as she stopped to admire a cluster of pink and white dogwood trees. They stood with the tall old oaks, hickories, and maples that had

2

witnessed Atlanta's growth from a small town called Termanis to a modern international city that played host to major corporate events, national political conventions and top-rank athletic competitions.

She had almost reached the corner when muffled shouts rose in the distance. She slowed her pace and tried to make out the words. The voices were chanting something — a low consistent hum. "Stop," she heard, but the rest of the chant ran together, indistinguishable. As she rounded the corner, Karen understood.

"Stop killing unborn babies! Stop killing unborn babies!"

The receptionist had warned her that pro-life demonstrators were picketing in front of the clinic.

"They've been out there twice a week for the last two months!" Cynthia Giles had said. "So don't be surprised if they're here when you arrive. Just get inside as fast as possible."

Karen approached with trepidation. She elbowed through a narrow gap in the crowd, but stopped short when she saw the solid line of picketers blocking the doors of the large, old, two-story house that housed the Downtown Women's Clinic. She spotted the red-headed police officer who had driven by only moments ago. He and three other police officers were standing in front of the picketers. Suddenly a new wave of excitement rolled through the crowd and Karen was caught in the crush of bodies.

"Move please!"

The voice came from behind Karen. She turned and saw three women hurrying toward her at a very fast pace.

3

"Please!" the dark-haired taller woman said.

Karen stepped aside as the three women strode past. Without warning, a hand reached out of the crowd and pushed the dark-haired woman so forcefully that she lost her balance. She tried to regain her footing, but the hand pushed her again. As she began to fall she released the arm of the younger woman.

"Get her inside, Betty." Her voice was strong and commanding.

A short stocky man was standing over the woman. His face was twisted and only a shade or two away from being purple.

"You ought to be ashamed of yourself, Jordan." His hands were tight fists at his sides. "You're doing the devil's work."

Karen watched in horror as he drew his leg back, gathering momentum before he smashed a heavily booted foot into the side of the woman's left leg. She clutched her thigh, her face contorted in pain. He was about to kick her again, and without thinking, Karen shoved the man as hard as she could. He stumbled and wavered for a moment.

The woman was on her feet with her eyes glued on her assailant. "You bastard. I want you arrested."

"You're all under arrest." It was the red-headed policeman again. He and four other officers had surrounded Karen, the woman and the purple-faced man. Before Karen could protest, strong hands were dragging her along the fringes of the noisy crowd.

"Wait a minute," she shouted. "I haven't done anything!"

"She assaulted me," the stocky man said. "You saw that, didn't you?"

One of the policemen began to read all three their rights. They were charged with inciting to riot.

The woman looked calm — much too calm for the situation. "Can't you do something to stop this?" Karen asked her.

"I'm afraid not." Green eyes held the slightest hint of a smile. "I've never been able to stop it before, and this is my seventh time."

"Your seventh time!" Karen was stunned. "Why would you put yourself in this situation more than once?"

"Hold it. I'd like to ask you a few questions for our listeners." Karen recognized the tall blond man as Chris Martin from Channel 2. She fully expected the police to clear him and his camera crew out of their way. "It will just take a minute, Officer."

Karen stared in amazement. "I don't believe this." She looked at the policeman. "You're going to stop for the TV camera?"

The officer scowled at her. "Just keep quiet. You don't need any more trouble than you're already in."

"Doctor Jordan, will the women's clinic continue to perform abortions despite your most recent arrest?"

"The clinic won't close or change its policies because of protesters who want to deny women control over their own bodies." Doctor Jordan's voice was firm and level.

"And what about you, Miss?" Chris Martin shoved the microphone in front of Karen. "What's your connection with the women's clinic? Did you come here today for an abortion?"

Karen felt a mixture of anger and terror. The whole fiasco was being taped for the evening news. Phillip would be furious.

"Did you come here for an abortion?" he repeated.

"That's none of your business." Karen managed to keep her voice steady.

"It is so his business," the stocky man shouted at Karen. "You tried to kill me. They've got it all on tape. Isn't that right, Chris?"

Chris Martin and the camera crew moved to the man's side. The reporter held out the microphone.

"My name is Tom O'Brien and I'm against the baby-killing. I'm against women doing away with babies who can't defend themselves." He pointed a chubby finger at Doctor Jordan. "She's the ringleader of the whole shebang. Who knows how many babies she's killed in the name of pro-choice. Pro-choice, hell. It's nothing but murder."

Karen felt a strong desire to slap him and all the other Tom O'Briens of the world.

"And that one — the skinny one — she's a lot more dangerous than she looks. Don't let her size fool you. She almost killed me. You must have it on tape. I just may charge her with assault."

For the first time Karen saw the mask of serenity fade from Chris Martin's face. "Yes, sir. I believe we have the entire incident on tape. In fact, I wanted to ask you why you kicked Doctor Jordan. She was on the ground at the time."

Tom O'Brien's face was turning purple again.

"Who said I kicked her? I never touched the woman. She's lying."

"Okay," one of the policemen said. "You can tell your stories to the judge. Right now, you're all going downtown." He looked at the officer who was standing beside Tom O'Brien. "You'd better take him in the other van. I'll take the women in this one." He put his hand on Doctor Jordan's shoulder. "Okay, ladies, into the van." He turned. "Any more comments out of you, mister, and we'll take you in as a nut case." Tom O'Brien took several steps backward without speaking another word.

Chris Martin and his crew were left standing in the middle of the crowded street.

Karen felt sick to her stomach. The coldness of the van's narrow metal bench reached through the thinness of her summer slacks and added to her general discomfort. The entire incident had the feel of a bad dream. She heard a solid click. Something hard pinched her left wrist, and she saw that she had been handcuffed to Doctor Jordan.

"Oh come on, Officer!" Karen was angry and annoyed. "Do I really look that dangerous?"

"I'm sorry, Miss." The policeman sounded sincere. "We don't have a choice. The book says we have to transport people in handcuffs. I'm not saying it makes sense, but it is the law."

"I'm Joanna Jordan." The dark-haired woman was looking at her intently. "Thank you for stepping in back there. Another kick like that might have fractured a rib."

"You're welcome." Karen took her first real look

7

at Joanna Jordan. She was tall and thin with dark wavy hair and expressive green eyes that reminded Karen of fine jade. "I think I was supposed to report to you this morning. I'm Karen Wainwright. I'm your new nurse for clinic on Mondays and Wednesdays."

"That's right. Cynthia told me you'd be here today." She raised an eyebrow. "This hasn't turned out to be a great introduction for you. I hope we haven't scared you off."

"That depends." Karen was worried. "How long do the police usually hold you when you're arrested? And who do I need to call to get out?"

"The clinic has an attorney. I'm sure Cynthia has already called her. She'll be here to get us out in about an hour." Joanna Jordan's voice was soothing. "You should be home for dinner."

The thought of home reminded Karen of Phillip and the TV news crew. Maybe the station wouldn't show the footage with her in it. Sure, she thought, and maybe they'll elect me President of the United States. How did she get herself into this mess?

"You're awfully pale," Joanna Jordan said. "Are you all right?"

"I'll be fine. I was just thinking of how my husband is going to react. He isn't the most liberal person in the world." She checked her watch. The pinch of the handcuffs and the weight of Joanna Jordan's arm added to her anxiety. "I have to pick my children up just after three."

Joanna Jordan nodded. "I don't think that will be a problem. You should be out in plenty of time to get your kids."

Joanna's green eyes sparkled with daring. They

8

had a somewhat disquieting effect on Karen and were anything but reassuring.

"I wish you'd tell me that I won't be arrested again if I continue to volunteer for the clinic."

"Would you believe me if I told you that?" A smile played in Joanna's eyes.

Karen took a deep breath. "No. I don't think so."

Joanna nodded. "Well, I can't promise you that anyway. But I can promise you that your life from this point on will not be dull."

CHAPTER 2

"I'm sorry this is taking so long." Joanna Jordan paced back and forth in the small cell. "It didn't occur to me that Jeannie might be out of town. I can't believe we've been in here almost three hours." She took a deep breath and exhaled slowly. "Vicki should be here in an hour."

"Are you sure she won't mind putting up my bail money? I could call Phillip if there's a problem."

Joanna thought Karen seemed remarkably relaxed for a woman who had been arrested and jailed for the first time in her life.

Joanna sat down on the bottom bunk across from her and was silent for a moment. There was something familiar about this woman. What was it? Perhaps she had seen her before at some medical meeting. She studied Karen, hoping to find a clue. She was tall and slender; her light brown hair was short, neat and wavy. A cleft in her chin added a dash of defiance to an already interesting face.

"It won't be any trouble," Joanna said. "Vicki has to come downtown to get me. Bailing you out at the same time will take all of another ten minutes." She watched as Karen rested her back against the rough cinderblock wall. Her red blouse and white slacks were a colorful relief from the solid grayness of the tiny cell.

"I appreciate that. I can give you a check as soon as the police return my pocketbook."

"That's not necessary. The clinic maintains a fund for bail and legal fees." Joanna stretched out on the thin mattress and propped her head on one elbow. "Since you're a volunteer at the clinic, our fund will cover you."

"That's the first good news I've had since I parked my car this morning." Karen's smile was like a magnet. "The law of averages had to be in my favor — eventually."

Joanna liked Karen's sense of humor. If she had to spend time in a cell, thank God it wasn't with a self-righteous do-gooder, or worse yet, a whiner. "This is not a usual day at the clinic. Honest." She made the sign of the cross over her heart. "Unfortunately, we've been an anti-choice target on and off for the past two months. But even they take a break sometimes."

11

"Good, because I can't honestly say I'm crazy about demonstrations and picket lines," Karen said. "I'm not sure I'm dedicated enough to do this on a regular basis. Not to mention the fact that my husband would divorce me for conduct unbecoming to his wife."

"He'll probably be proud of you for standing up for what you believe."

Karen laughed and shook her head. "I'm afraid not. Phillip doesn't like anything controversial, and getting arrested certainly ranks in that category."

Joanna had not expected Karen's response. "In that case, I'm surprised you volunteered for the clinic. We've certainly been in the news on a regular basis for the last few months."

Karen raised an eyebrow. "Listen, if I only did what Phillip approved of, I'd rarely leave the house. This was a compromise. I told him I wanted to volunteer at the women's prison once a week. He suggested I volunteer for something closer, so when I chose the women's clinic, he could hardly complain too loudly. Although he did say he'd rather I volunteer my time at a children's hospital."

"Why did you choose the clinic?" Joanna was curious about this woman who looked as if sorting the family laundry was the most difficult decision she had ever had to make.

"I'm not absolutely sure." Karen stretched out on her bunk, her body parallel to Joanna's. "My life has been taking unexpected turns for the past year. Nothing monumental or anything. Most of my friends haven't even noticed. But . . ." She rubbed her earlobe. "I know there's a difference. I want to be more involved in things I only watched on the news

12

before." She grinned. "I joined Greenpeace, the American Civil Liberties Union, the Sierra Club, Save the Animals, and a few more I can't think of right now." Joanna was captivated by Karen's apparent comfort with unguarded openness. "I'm tired of watching life from the sidelines. I want to be involved in things that matter, and I can't think of anything that's more basic, or more important, than the right to make a choice about what happens to one's own body. I'm no historian, but it seems to me that any society that tries to control what its citizens think starts first by trying to control their bodies in small ways. The way the Nazis tried in World War Two. They decided who could marry and who could have children. Women didn't really have a choice. The state decided everything for the good of the state." She stopped talking and for a moment Joanna felt as if Karen's eyes were locked on her own. She was aware of an energy that passed between them. "I didn't mean to get so philosophical. You're very easy to talk to. I feel as if we've known each other for years." She smiled. "Maybe that's what going to jail with someone does for people."

Joanna laughed. "I don't think so. I've been to jail on four other occasions and we never shared more than a cell."

"Well whatever it is, I like it," Karen declared. "But I don't want to do all the talking. It's your turn. Why are you working at a women's clinic? And why are you willing to go to jail on the issue of choice?"

"I'm a physician. I'm simply taking care of my patients." Joanna spoke her stock reply.

"Oh come on! If that was all it took, jails would

be filled with physicians. I remember seeing you on the news, but I can't remember one other physician getting arrested in Atlanta." She tilted her head and looked at Joanna in silence for a moment. "If you don't want to tell me, I understand, but please don't patronize me. I'm really interested. To paraphrase you, any belief that's strong enough to go to jail for is worth understanding."

"Touché!" Karen's candor caught Joanna by surprise. She had given the same reply so many times she had almost lost touch with the honest answer. It lay under years of defenses, deep and hidden, all but forgotten, as dangerous as it ever was. It lay coiled inside her, ferocious truth, ready to spring, to deal stark reality and tear away delusions.

"I'm not sure I can answer the question in twenty-five words or less," Joanna said. For some reason she couldn't explain, she trusted Karen. Maybe it was her openness, her willingness to risk her inner world with Joanna. Joanna *knew*, without having to hear the words, that Karen didn't share her inner life with everyone she met. Joanna would take the same risk. If the future proved her decision faulty, so be it.

"If you get tired of listening, stop me." Joanna smiled.

Karen made a sweeping gesture. "Consider me a captive audience."

Joanna felt complimented by Karen's attention. It added to her sense of trust. "I can't remember a time when I didn't want to be a doctor," Joanna began. "I was always bringing some hurt animal home to take care of." Pictures of the past tumbled through Joanna's mind. "My mother was a nurse, and she helped me take care of the winners and the losers from hundreds of dog-and-cat fights. When I look back now, I realize how wonderfully patient she was with me. At one point we had three dogs, two cats, and four baby sparrows to take care of at once." The memory brought a smile, and a touch of sadness. "My mother would come home after working a full shift at the hospital, fix dinner and do whatever else needed to be done, and then spend an hour or more helping me nurse whatever animals I'd carried home that week."

"It sounds as if you two were very close." Karen's gaze was soft and kind. "You said she *was* a nurse. Is she still alive?"

"No." Joanna still felt the weight of her mother's loss. "She got sick when I was eleven. All of a sudden she was pale, and tired. The next thing I knew she was in bed because she didn't feel well. I was afraid to ask her what was wrong. I guess somehow I knew how serious it was for someone as active as she was to be too tired to do any of the things she enjoyed before. The day she finally told me she was dying, I cried for a long time. She held me and said that some day doctors would find a cure for the cancer that was killing her, that medicine just wasn't advanced enough to save her. That's when I actually thought the words for the first time — I'll be a doctor so I can help people get well again. I was going to tell her the next day. I never got the chance. She died during the night. I wish I could have been with her."

"You must have been very frightened," Karen said. "It would be awful not to have a chance to say good-bye."

15

"I was frightened, but at least I had my family. My sister and I were very close. We became even closer in the months and years that followed."

"How about your father? Were you close to him?"

Joanna fought the desire to change the subject. "My father never saw much reason to develop a relationship with me or my sister. He truly believed that daughters were what you ended up with if you weren't lucky enough to have another son." She fought harder against the urge to push the memories back and talk of lighter and happier times. "His attitude brought Eileen and me even closer. It was us against the world. When my father said he had no intention of sending me to medical school, that he had two sons to send to college, Eileen tried to get him to change his mind. He wouldn't budge. If I wanted to be a nurse, he *might* consider that, but it was ridiculous to think of sending a girl to medical school when she'd just drop out and raise kids as soon as some guy asked her to marry him."

"Did he get any better as you got older?" Karen's voice was soft.

"No." Joanna felt frozen with remembered anger. She could feel the blood draining from her face.

"Are you all right, Joanna?" Karen's voice broke through the ice. "You're as white as a ghost." She stared at Joanna. "I didn't mean to get you upset. If you'd rather not talk about this, I understand."

Joanna pushed herself to go on past the years of silence, through the tunnels of hidden pain, through narrow passages devoid of all warmth. "My father was responsible for Eileen's death." Karen didn't blink. "She was seventeen when she became pregnant. She wanted an abortion and went to our family doctor for help." She could feel the hot wetness of tears as they rolled silently down her cheeks. "That was a mistake. He was a member of my father's church. He called my father and told him about Eileen." She brushed the tears away with her hand. "He told her she'd have to have the baby, that it was bad enough she'd disgraced him, she was not going to disgrace him further by killing the baby." Joanna took a deep breath. "Eileen begged him to reconsider, but he wouldn't budge. He kept telling her to beg God's forgiveness for disgracing her family. That night on the way to choir practice, she drove her car off a bridge. The medical examiner said she was killed instantly. My father said God had punished her and saved our family from humiliation. But God didn't have anything to do with it. Eileen committed suicide because he wouldn't let her terminate a pregnancy that was a stupid teenage mistake."

Joanna could feel her hands shaking as she wiped the tears from her face. "I'm sorry." She inhaled deeply in an effort to regain her composure. "I'm afraid the subject is still too painful for me." She swallowed hard to slow the flow of tears. "I'm not sure it will ever be different. It hasn't changed much in all these years."

Tears rose up in Karen's eyes like pools fed by an underground stream. The thin curtain they formed hid nothing of the compassion that was so clearly present, and Joanna felt deeply touched. It was the first time she could remember anyone shedding tears because of her pain, the first time she had felt so close to someone so fast. In the passing of an instant, Joanna *knew* that this woman

17

was unlike any she had known before. Her heart pounded a drumbeat in her ears. She wanted to put her arms around Karen, to hold her close with exquisite tenderness.

"I'm so sorry, Joanna. I wish I could have been there to comfort you."

Karen's words struck the core of Joanna's heart and set her hands trembling anew. She urged herself to think again of Eileen; those feelings were less threatening than what she felt for Karen.

"Thank you for caring." Joanna smiled at Karen. "I appreciate it more than you know." She forced her thoughts away from Karen. "I focused all my time and energy on winning a scholarship to college and medical school. I was determined to do something for all the Eileens in the world."

Karen shook her head. "That's why you're at the clinic, and why you're sitting in a jail cell now."

Joanna felt warmed by Karen's understanding. *How easy it would be to love this woman.* The thought came and went like lightning, leaving the taste of fear in its wake.

"I guess so, Karen. But I could do very well without the trips to jail. This is definitely not my idea of fun." She wanted to change the subject and the mood.

There was the sound of something light and metallic hitting the concrete floor farther up the cell block.

Karen jumped and caught her breath. Her eyes were wide with fright and the color was gone from her face. "I'm not generally a nervous person, but this place gives me the creeps." She sat up against the cinderblock wall again.

"I know what you mean," Joanna said. "I feel terrible about your involvement in this."

Karen's smile was warm and reassuring. "Hey, you're not responsible for my arrest." She grinned widely. "This will be an exciting story to tell my grandchildren some day, but right now all the awful prison movies I've ever seen on late-night television are replaying in my head. I keep imagining some six-foot-six Swedish lesbian named Dagmar knocking on our cell door and telling me I'm moving in with her to do my time."

Joanna laughed. "Not a pleasant thought. If it helps any, when Dagmar shows up, I'll try to talk her into keeping you for just a week."

"I can't tell you how much that means to me. I feel so much better knowing you'll protect me." Karen's mock sarcasm turned to laughter.

There was the sound of rattling keys and a large black woman was standing in front of the cell.

"Okay, ladies, pipe down. This isn't a fun house." She opened the cell door. "Come on out, you two. You've got your walking papers."

Vicki Richardson was waiting just outside the booking room. She hugged Joanna. "Are you all right?"

"Other than a badly bruised thigh, I'm fine." She looked at Vicki's impeccable white suit, her subtle makeup, her matching shoes and handbag, and thought how unnatural she looked in an inner city police station. The reason she was there didn't seem to matter — Vicki didn't fit in or near any situation

19

that wasn't strictly upper middle class. Even at Emory University, where old money was definitely comfortable, and where Vicki held a tenured professorship in chemistry, she seemed out of place. Not that she tried to be different, she didn't. She didn't have to try. Joanna had reached that conclusion almost twelve years ago when they first met. The department had recommended Vicki as a tutor for organic chemistry, the only course in Joanna's entire college and medical school career that had ever given her a problem. Vicki, a tall skinny senior with a disdain for any student dumb enough to need her services, had pulled Joanna through organic chemistry with an "A." They began dating with a celebration of Joanna's success, and became lovers four weeks later.

Joanna put her hand on Karen's shoulder. "Vicki Richardson, this is my partner in crime, Karen Wainwright."

Vicki extended her hand toward Karen. "I've heard all about your little incident this morning. I hope it won't change your mind about volunteering for the clinic. Lord knows, they need help. The patients are like rabbits. They're either pregnant or recovering from an abortion. If you ask me, the better part of valor would be to sterilize all of them. It would save taxpayers millions."

Karen's mouth was slightly open, and her eyes were riveted on Vicki.

"You'll have to get used to Vicki." Joanna smiled. "I'm sure she was royalty in more than one past life."

"Never mind my past lives. We need to get out of downtown Atlanta before the five o'clock rush hour."

20

She took Joanna's arm and started toward the door. "Do we need to drop you somewhere?" She spoke over her shoulder, in Karen's general direction.

"I'd appreciate a ride to my car. I'm in the clinic's parking lot." Karen followed them. "I hope I never see this place again."

Vicki looked at Joanna. "Well, if we predict the future by what has taken place in the past, those who associate themselves with the Downtown Women's Clinic have a better than average chance on any given day of ending up in jail."

Joanna was sorry to see Karen go when they dropped her off at her car. The trip home always seemed longer than the fifteen minutes it required if one stayed within the posted speed limit on Atlanta's residential streets. Joanna rarely exceeded the speed limit and when she did, it was by accident. Today, the trip seemed even longer. She hated the long silences that had become a usual part of her shared ride with Vicki.

She was aware of the hard coolness of the steering wheel against her warm hands. One of life's many contrasts, she thought.

The light ahead turned red and she slowed the car to a stop. She could see Vicki in the edges of her peripheral vision. Her face was turned to the window and she was very still.

"I'm sorry you had to come downtown to bail me out." Joanna laid her hand lightly on Vicki's arm. "I know how much you hate to get called away during the day."

21

Vicki looked at Joanna. "I think you know I would never leave you sitting in a cell one minute longer than necessary. If I could have gotten there sooner, I would have."

The light turned green and Joanna put most of her attention back on the road. "I thought you might still be angry about last night." She glanced quickly at Vicki. "I wasn't positive you'd come get me out."

"Really, Joanna." Vicki sounded exasperated. "You'd think you just met me. When in the last twelve years have I not come when you said you needed help?"

Joanna started to name the two incidents that stood out in her mind but decided it would only fuel the fires.

"As far as last night is concerned," Vicki continued, "I've given up on getting you to understand that this clinic business can do you permanent damage. You're a big girl, and if you want to throw your career down the drain, no one can stop you. I just don't understand why you have to align yourself with unpopular causes. Hell, I don't see why you have to have a cause to fight for anyhow. It's not as if you couldn't be doing something else."

"You knew I was a cause person when you met me." Joanna felt slightly defensive. "I never pretended to be anything else."

"Sure, I knew, but I thought you'd mellow with time. I thought eventually you'd want a regular practice." She put her arm around Joanna's shoulders and rested her hand gently against the side of her neck. "I talked to Donna Cassidy this morning. She asked me to remind you that her offer

22

of a full partnership is still open. She has almost twice the number of patients that she can handle comfortably." Vicki ran her fingers slowly along the back of Joanna's neck. "It would be nice to have you in an area where arrests weren't a constant threat." She ran her fingers through Joanna's hair and massaged the back of her head. "I wish you'd give it some serious thought."

"Donna Cassidy would be the last person I'd go into practice with. She's so strung out she's lucky she can find her way to her office. I wouldn't want her treating me or any of my patients."

"An awful lot of people disagree with you." Vicki's voice was beginning to take on an edge. "She's well respected in the medical community. She'll probably be the next president of the Georgia Medical Association."

"I'm not saying she's not a bright woman," Joanna said. "She's very bright and politically sophisticated." She bit back her contempt. "She's also overworked and only marginally aware of what's going on in her practice. Her patients may as well be on a conveyor belt. She's hand-in-glove with the pharmaceutical companies and doesn't even know what she's prescribed half the time. It's irresponsible. A lot of her patients are taking four and five different new drugs." Joanna was furious that any physician would treat patients in such a way, and furious that Vicki would hold Donna Cassidy up as a role model. "I don't need her problems."

"At least when she makes the news, it's for something she can be proud of. I doubt she's ever seen the inside of a jail cell."

Joanna parked in front of the large tri-level

23

house that had been home to them for almost eleven years. Its old brick exterior and matching eight-foot wall blended into the rustic landscape of ivy-covered trees and yards, towering hardwoods and tall, well-shaped pines.

Vicki took her arm pleadingly. "I'm really very tired of worrying about you getting hurt, or worse yet, blown up by some crackpot who's convinced you're doing the work of the devil. Haven't you already done your part for the cause? Let someone else contribute something. For us, if nothing else, get out of the clinic."

Joanna felt totally frustrated. "You really don't understand, Vicki. I know you mean well, but you have no idea what you're trying to get me into."

"Will you at least think about getting out of the clinic?"

Maybe it's the only way to save our relationship, Joanna thought. Twelve years was a long time. She looked at Vicki. "I'm not sure I could be happy in a regular practice. I've been involved in causes since I was fifteen."

"Fine," Vicki said. "Save the whales. Or march against people wearing fur coats. Just get out of the front line for a while."

"I'll give it some serious thought." But Joanna knew she'd avoid thinking about the subject unless Vicki brought it up again.

"Even if you got out for a couple of months, we could take a vacation," Vicki said. "I'd like some time with you, Joanna. I don't feel as if we know each other anymore. The only time I see you is when you're on your way to another meeting for abortion rights." Her voice cracked with emotion. She

24

put her hand on Joanna's cheek and brushed it tenderly. "I miss you. I miss us."

"I really will think about it, Vicki, but I can't just quit. Even if I wanted to get out, I have obligations." Joanna felt pressured, a feeling she definitely disliked. Why didn't Vicki give up this approach? It never worked, and it never would. Vicki leaned over and kissed her on the cheek. "All right. I'll take you at your word. Just think about it."

Phillip's car was in the driveway when Karen pulled in. She looked at her watch — 5:45 pm. If he had followed his usual pattern, he had already tuned in the early evening newscast on WSB-TV. She took a deep breath and exhaled slowly. Maybe she wasn't included in the footage they aired. Slim chance, she thought. She might as well beard the lion in his den.

The house, a rambling, brick, two-story set fifty yards back from the street, looked out over well-manicured lawns and neatly pruned shrubbery and trees. It was relatively new, less than twenty years old, well constructed and typical for its rising middle-class neighborhood. The air in the hallway was cooler, and she could hear the television in the kitchen. Phillip would be seated at the kitchen table, drinking a glass of lemonade, his eyes glued to the set. If he had seen it, there was nothing she could do but face him. She bolstered her courage and walked into the kitchen.

"Hi. Are the boys home?" She exerted a conscious effort to keep her voice light.

Phillip turned toward her and she knew immediately that he had seen the footage of her at the clinic. His face was scarlet and the veins in his left temple were swollen and drawn tight, like guitar strings.

Karen felt total resignation. Whatever would happen now, it was too late to change anything. It wasn't so terrible anyway. It wasn't as if she had been photographed robbing a bank, or marching for the young Nazi Party. She put her pocketbook on the utility island in front of the sink and braced herself emotionally.

Phillip's mouth was moving but there was no sound. She had the feeling that she was watching a silent movie.

Phillip was shaking his head. He had one of his best "how could you?" expressions on his face. Suddenly the sound was back. "Are you deliberately trying to embarrass the boys and me? For God's sake, Karen, don't you care that we have to live with the fallout of your involvement with that abortion clinic? They mentioned you in the same breath with Doctor Joanna Jordan. I asked you not to get involved with those people. Maybe now you'll believe that I know what I'm talking about."

"It's not an abortion clinic," Karen said. "It's a women's clinic. They treat all ages and all kinds of women's medical problems."

Phillip's expression was incredulous. "And you don't care how it affects your sons or your husband? You'll suit yourself no matter how it hurts your family?"

Overwhelmed, she sat down across from Phillip. She much preferred Phillip's anger to his

26

how-could-you-do-this-to-the-boys-and-me routine. This tack always lasted longer, and she never seemed able to mount an adequate response to suit him. For that matter, her responses never even convinced her. Maybe she *was* a bad mother and wife.

"Surely you have something to say?" Phillip's tone was a mixture of sarcasm and self-pity. "You owe us that much. After all, I love you." His voice got even stickier. "And you are the boys' mother."

Those words always worked magic for Phillip, because no matter what the strength of Karen's resolve to confront him on his manipulative behavior, "you are the boys' mother" sucked it out of her like a dog sucking the marrow from bones. It was always the same. She was left with a hollow feeling, the sense that she was missing something essential, the core quality that gave an individual unique value. She had entered her marriage with the nagging fear that Phillip and the world would discover that she was emotionally and spiritually bankrupt, although he had never actually said, "Look, Karen, you have nothing to give to a relationship, nothing except your willingness to be of service to your family. You're good at housework and laundry, and taking the boys to football practice. Why not just accept it and give what you can? Be a good wife and a good mother."

"I don't think I'm asking too much." The self-pity escalated. "I just want you to put the boys and me first in your life."

The words were almost more than Karen could bear. She had never struck anyone, but here and now, she wanted to slap Phillip. She clenched her fists and leaned toward him. "I did that for the past sixteen years." Her voice trembled with anger. "I

27

quit my job at Saint Joseph's to be with Brad and Eric when they were babies. 'Just stay home until they're old enough for the first grade,' you said." Karen could feel her fury growing like a fanned flame. "When I wanted to go back to work you thought I should stay home until the boys were ready for the fourth grade. Then it was wait until they're in high school." She could feel her nails digging into her palms. "Well, I waited, and I waited . . . Brad and Eric are juniors, and you still can't make up your mind whether being a 'good mother' at this point means staying home or going back to work."

"That's ridiculous," Phillip snapped. "I told you four months ago that it would help if you went back to work. We need the extra money to help pay their college tuition. You think it's been easy being the only financial support for the family? The boys needed a full-time mother." His condescension was fast becoming self-righteousness. "I've been busting my ass for years while you sat home or went to women's clubs. Now just because I pointed out that it would help if you went back to work, you act as if I'm asking you to dig ditches. Anyone would think that a person who spent four years getting a bachelor's degree in nursing would want to use what she's learned." His eyes narrowed but his voice had softened. "Damn it, Karen, I know it hasn't been a vacation for sixteen years, but all you want to do now is volunteer work."

Karen's heart was beating wildly. Her temples pounded. "Don't you ever listen? I can't just walk back into a hospital and start taking care of patients. Nursing has moved light years since I quit.

Technology is different, medications are different, priorities are different. If I'd gone back when Brad and Eric started school, or even when they were in the fourth grade, it would have been different . . . now the most I can hope for is volunteer work until I can catch up with all the changes. So don't you dare tell me I don't want to work. You didn't want me to go back until you found out how much better the salaries are now."

"Well, does it have to be at that damned abortion clinic? Why can't you volunteer with children?"

"I could, Phillip, but that would get me into pediatric nursing, and pediatric nursing doesn't pay anywhere near what OB/GYN will pay once I've caught on again."

"Oh." Phillip looked as if a twenty-watt bulb had been turned on in his head. "I just hope it doesn't take you too long. We need the money."

She was about to respond when the front door slammed. Eric and Brad were home.

"We're in the kitchen, boys," Phillip called.

Karen watched her sons as they poured themselves a glass of lemonade. They had been only two weeks old when Phillip and Karen adopted them. The agency had seemed pleased that they were willing to take a set of fraternal twins. That was sixteen years ago, and Eric was now an inch taller than Brad, with darker and curlier hair. He had an even temper and an easygoing attitude.

Eric bent over and kissed Karen on the cheek. "Hi, Mom. Jimmy Storr's mother said you got arrested today for marching for abortion rights, or something like that. Did you?"

"God, Mom, this is really embarrassing. Do you

29

have to get involved in these weird deals?" Brad leaned against the kitchen island as he talked. He was exceptionally handsome with dark brown eyes and long thick lashes. "Nobody else's mom gets involved in stuff like that."

Karen felt attacked on all sides. Even more devastating were the feelings of failure and inadequacy. Maybe Phillip was right. Maybe she was a bad mother. But even good mothers embarrassed their teenagers.

"Well, Mom?" Brad's tone was almost identical to Phillip's. "Did you really get yourself arrested?"

"Not exactly." Karen felt defensive. "I was arrested because I pushed a man who was kicking a woman he had already knocked down. He could have hurt her badly."

"Wow! You got into a street fight?" Eric asked, awed.

Brad's expression was one of disgust. "If that had been me, you would have had a fit. Do us a favor, Mom, if you have to get involved with any more crazy causes, at least stay out of jail."

While there was a note of humor, finally, in Brad's voice, Karen felt panic. She scanned Phillip's face. A smirk curled at the corners of his mouth. His reddish blond hair had begun to thin more than a year ago, and Karen watched as Phillip stroked his beard. It was a habit that annoyed her since she realized that it usually happened when he felt justified and self-satisfied. The knowledge fueled a small rebellion inside her.

She eyed Brad. "I'm not willing to quit my volunteer time with the women's clinic. I believe in what I'm doing and I want to help women with their special problems."

"Oh that's just great, Mom." Brad's voice was dripping with sarcasm and anger. "You don't really care about us at all."

Eric looked confused.

"I care very much. I love you." Karen wanted peace with her sons. "I'm sorry you were embarrassed, but life doesn't always fit into neat little packages. Sometimes standing up for a conviction is costly. This was one of those times."

"Well I think the whole thing is dumb." Brad's words were emphatic. "Even my friends know what to do so nobody gets pregnant." He looked at his father as if for reassurance, then back at Karen.

Karen felt physically sick. She was losing Brad to Phillip's prejudices. If she lost the battle to teach Brad to think for himself, Brad could easily grow into a carbon copy of Phillip.

"Why do you want to help women who don't know any better than to get pregnant in the first place?" Brad's mouth tightened into a thin red line, but Karen saw the hurt in his eyes. "I think you're dumb for getting arrested for them."

"That's enough, son." Phillip spoke decisively. "Don't talk to your mother like that."

"I'm going upstairs." Brad started for the door. "You ought to tell her that what she's doing doesn't look very good."

"Shut up, Brad." Eric took several steps toward his brother.

Brad spun around and held up a clenched fist. "Make me!"

31

"That's enough from both of you." Phillip raised his voice for the first time. He looked at Karen. "I'm sure your mother understands what she's doing, and maybe she'll change her mind."

Not this time, Karen thought. I'm not giving in on this one. She looked at her sons. "I don't plan to get arrested again," she said. "But if something does happen, I'll certainly reevaluate the situation." She looked directly into Phillip's eyes. "I'm staying at the clinic. It's my way back to nursing."

The words are easy, she thought. I hope I have the strength to stand by them.

CHAPTER 3

Joanna Jordan loved the early morning hours when the streets of Atlanta were quiet and deserted. The stillness had a calming effect on her that lasted even through her frequently hectic days.

She habitually arrived before 6:00 a.m. to read over the cases scheduled for surgery and to review files of women returning for post-surgical visits. She had promised herself in medical school that if she ever reached the point where her patients were just diagnoses and numbers, she would take a long vacation, and if that didn't put things back into perspective, she would leave medicine. She counted herself lucky that she had never come close to needing that self-imposed break. Several of her friends had gone beyond that boundary without any insight into their own problems. Donna Cassidy was at a crisis point and didn't even realize it. Joanna had tried to talk with her, but Donna wasn't hearing any of it.

Joanna headed from her car to the clinic's back door. Two street lights and the glow from a full moon gave the only light to the early morning hour. As she started to climb the back porch steps, a shadow slid into her field of vision. She froze mid-step as her heartbeat quickened and pounded against her chest. Her mind raced through her options. The car was locked — and thirty yards away — car keys at the bottom of her handbag.

The shadow moved again in the darkness. Vicki's warning tumbled through her mind: "It's too dangerous to be at the clinic by yourself so early. You could get mugged and lie there for hours before anyone found you."

It's too late to run, she thought. She could feel tiny beads of perspiration on her forehead and upper lip. Her heart raced wildly as she summoned every bit of her courage and called out, "Who's there? The clinic doesn't open until eight."

"It's me, Joanna." The voice was vaguely familiar. "Karen Wainwright." She stepped into a pool of light.

Joanna took a deep breath and let her muscles relax as she exhaled. She ran a hand across her forehead; the perspiration felt cold and wet.

Suddenly, as quickly as it had appeared, her relief gave way to annoyance. "You almost scared me to death." Joanna spoke angrily as she climbed the porch stairs, Karen scurrying after her. "Don't you know better than to hide in the shadows like that?" Joanna was face to face with her now, and her eyes moved along the soft yellow borders of moonlight that bathed Karen's eyes and hair.

"I'm sorry, I didn't mean to scare you." Karen sounded contrite. "I should have called to you when you were getting out of your car."

Joanna exhaled loudly. "It's okay. My pulse is almost back to normal." She turned the key in the lock. "Come in quickly. I have to turn the alarm off." She took several steps, clicked on the light, and punched the code to disarm the security system.

"There." She turned to Karen and smiled. "I'm sorry if I sounded gruff, but you really scared the daylights out of me. I could use some coffee, how about you?" She walked toward the kitchen without waiting for a response. "What in the world are you doing here this early? Won't your family be worried about you?"

"I told them last night that I'd be leaving for the clinic early." She followed Joanna to the coffee machine. "We're all up early."

Joanna watched Karen out of the corner of her eye as she poured sugar and creamer into a mug.

"When I spoke with your receptionist yesterday, she said you're usually here by six. I thought you might be able to use a little help."

Joanna looked at Karen with increasing interest.

Her eyes held secrets Joanna wanted to remember. The clear blue color was not merely attractive, it was comfortable.

"I hope you don't mind," Karen said. "I hope I'm not intruding into time you've carved out for yourself. If I am, please say so."

Joanna only half heard what Karen was saying. She was trying again to identify what was so familiar about her. The coffee machine buzzed and Joanna turned her attention to the mug in front of her. "Help yourself."

"Thank you." Karen stood next to Joanna and spooned creamer and sugar into her cup.

Joanna was aware of the light sweet scent of Karen's cologne.

"Have I?" Karen's question broke into Joanna's thoughts.

"Have you what?"

"Have I interrupted time you've carved out for yourself?" Karen asked.

"No." Joanna took a small swallow of coffee. "I could use the help." She felt tinges of sexual excitement stir in her. More than that, she felt attracted on all levels. "I'm still a little surprised that anyone but me gets up this early."

"All the Wainwrights are early risers. Someone is always leaving early for something. Phillip leaves for the gym at five-thirty two or three times a week. The boys go with him, and they have breakfast together before he drops them off at school." She swallowed coffee. "I can be at the clinic at six on Mondays and Wednesdays if that's okay with you."

"That sounds great." Joanna caught Karen's eyes

and smiled. "Just don't jump out of the shadows again. I'm too young to die of fear-induced cardiac arrest."

"I'm really sorry about that. It won't happen again."

"We've had several threats against the clinic, and I've had several threats made against me personally. I'd be a lot more comfortable if I knew that the person waiting for me is you and not some nut who thinks he's doing God's work."

"That's terrible. Can't the police do something?" Karen looked horrified.

"There isn't much for them to go on." Joanna shrugged. "A man's muffled voice on the phone, a note with no return address . . . Actually, the police did manage to trace the calls twice, but they both came from a public phone at Lenox Square Mall."

"That certainly leaves a wide open field." Karen's face lost all hint of a smile. "It's too bad the man is that clever. I guess all you can do is hope he makes a mistake soon."

"I'm happy when we go several weeks without any new threats. But the whole idea of those kinds of nuts out there leaves me just a little on edge."

"Is there anything else I can do? I could manage one evening a week."

"We have a political action group that meets Thursday nights from seven to nine. We put out a newsletter every other month and lobby Congress on various issues." Joanna sipped from her mug. "We can always use more help."

"Perfect. Phillip and the boys go to a hiking club meeting every Thursday." Karen sounded excited.

Joanna opened a drawer and handed Karen a photocopied map. "This should get you to my home without any problems."

"Great." Karen glanced at the directions. "I'll be there."

CHAPTER 4

"Just a minute," Karen called. She opened the side door off her kitchen and found Ammie Driscal waiting impatiently. "Ammie, what are you doing out so early?" She looked at her watch. "It's only quarter after eight."

"I thought I'd bring you and the boys a cake." Ammie Driscal breezed past Karen and put the plate on the island in the middle of the kitchen. She was a tall, wiry woman with dark brown hair and a penchant for warm-up clothes and tennis. The lettering on the back of her light blue sweatshirt read ATLANTA'S BEST. "It's devil's food with chocolate icing. I got carried away with a new recipe and remembered that devil's food is your favorite." She sat down at the kitchen table. "Aren't you going to offer me some coffee?"

"I just made a fresh pot." Karen poured coffee for both of them and sat down across from her close friend. They had known each other since Ammie and her husband, Carl, moved to Atlanta from Mississippi fifteen years ago.

"Well?" Ammie's eyes were wide with excitement. "I want to hear the whole story about your day at the women's clinic."

Karen had wondered how long it would take before the questions started rolling in from the neighborhood. She was surprised Ammie hadn't phoned or stopped by last night. "If you saw the news you would know I didn't get to spend the day at the clinic. I got arrested before I even had a chance to get inside."

"Everybody in the subdivision saw the news," Ammie said. "It's *the* topic on the tennis courts. If people missed you on the six o'clock news, they caught you at eleven. CNN Headline News had you on every half hour. You're the biggest thing in the neighborhood since Sherman stormed Atlanta on his way to Savannah."

Karen looked at the childlike grin on Ammie's face and shook her head. "Somehow that doesn't make me feel very good about the whole thing." Karen hated gossip.

Ammie shrugged. "It's done now. You might as well enjoy it, everyone else is." Her eyes took on a new mischievousness. "With the exception of Carl, of course. Carl spent the evening mumbling something about 'poor Phillip,' and 'she ought to be horsewhipped.' He was still mumbling when he left for work. I'm sure he'll call Phillip later and offer his condolences. I wanted to come by last night, but he insisted on 'allowing Phillip to handle the retard,' whatever that means."

"God! You'd think I'd committed murder or treason." Karen couldn't remember the last time she felt this annoyed with anything or anybody.

"Murder or treason Carl could understand." Ammie's voice was replete with gravity. "Murder and treason are crimes in the Southern Gentleman's tradition. Making a spectacle of oneself in public, and on camera, is not."

They looked at each other and burst into peals of laughter. When they regained their composure, Karen filled Ammie in on what didn't get on the television news.

"Phillip will never forgive you," Ammie said through waves of intermittent laughter.

"It will just be a part of a long list of things he'll never forgive me for." Karen was resigned to Phillip's displeasure with anything she initiated or pursued on her own. "He'll just have to get used to me working at the clinic."

Ammie looked surprised. "You're going back?"

"Sure. It's perfect for brushing up on my clinical skills, and for getting involved in current issues."

"You must not have heard about Doctor Jordan." Ammie leaned forward and propped her chin on her hand.

41

"She seems like a very bright and caring person. I think I'll enjoy working with her." Karen refilled their cups. "What else is there that I should know?"

"The woman is an avowed lesbian. It's sort of an open secret. She's been living with some female chemistry professor who teaches at Emory University." Ammie looked as if she'd just made a present of the secret Coca-Cola formula to PepsiCo and was waiting for her reward.

"How do you know that's true?" Images of Joanna Jordan filled Karen's mind, and for an instant, she wondered what lovemaking would be like with her. "It sounds like more gossip to me." Karen resented this attack on someone she liked.

"Well, I haven't slept with her if that's what you mean, but Bonnie York's sister is one of those and she told Bonnie that she met Doctor Jordan and her friend at a party. According to her, they don't get along very well. It seems that the friend doesn't care for Doctor Jordan's involvement in causes. I can't say I blame her. Causes are bound to make martyrs out of those who lead them."

"We'd still be back in the Middle Ages if somebody hadn't stuck her neck out for women's rights." Karen didn't like Ammie's attitude toward Joanna. "I'm glad we have doctors like Joanna Jordan. She seems like a very caring person who really wants to make a difference in women's lives." She looked Ammie squarely in the eyes. "I admire her and the work she's doing for all women."

"Since when do you admire lesbians?" Ammie crossed her arms; her voice had taken on the sharp edge of a challenge.

"I've never really thought about it, but I probably

have admired women who are lesbians and I just didn't know it or even wondered about their private lives in their own bedrooms." Karen was disappointed. She wished Ammie wouldn't push a subject so unworthy of their time or attention, a subject that was making her increasingly uncomfortable. "What difference does it make who Joanna Jordan sleeps with? As long as I don't have to step over them in the aisles at Kroger, I couldn't care less."

"Well maybe you *should* care." Ammie sounded angry. "You've had an attitude problem ever since you started seeing that psychologist. You've gotten very argumentative. It certainly isn't a pleasant trait."

The few friends Karen had told about seeing Doctor Wade had used similar arguments to convince her that she should quit therapy. She had little tolerance for this argument anymore. She believed her therapist's comments regarding her friends' complaints.

"I think it's pretty standard for people in therapy to be seen by their friends as changed for the worse," Karen explained "According to Doctor Wade, as people get healthier, their friends have to accommodate the changes in their personalities. It can be a little threatening to people who had known the individual as a quiet person who seldom expressed an opinion."

"I don't feel threatened," Ammie retorted. "I feel like I'm watching a friend make mistakes that will cost her dearly in the future." Ammie's brown eyes softened. "I'm worried about you. You never complained about Phillip or your boys before you

43

started seeing this Doctor Wade. Suddenly you're a liberated woman who wants her family to just go along with whatever she wants." Ammie shook her head. "It isn't right, Karen. It just isn't right."

Karen felt her anger rising. This time she didn't stop it. "Bullshit! No one ever worried about how happy I was fulfilling Phillip's every wish, or how damaging it was to me to always put myself last." The more she thought about it, the angrier she became. "God, Ammie, I had lost touch with myself, I didn't even know what I felt anymore. I had allowed myself to become a non-person." She took a deep breath and closed her eyes for a moment. Why am I even bothering to tell her this, she thought. She won't understand. She looked at Ammie and was sorry she had said anything. "Look, let's just agree to disagree about Joanna Jordan and my work at the clinic. We just see it differently."

Ammie's face was almost stoic. "I guess you're right." She got to her feet. "Just be careful around Jordan. You never know about those people. I've heard most of them are oversexed."

Karen threw her arms up in a gesture of surrender. "I give up. You win. I'll watch myself very carefully. But since Joanna already has a lover and a whole group of women to choose from, if she wants a change, I don't think she'll be after me. And even if she was, I wouldn't be interested. I'm attracted to men, not women."

"Hell, I know you're not attracted to women," Ammie said. "I just want you to watch out for that Doctor Jordan."

44

"I'll be careful," Karen said. She felt her body tense as images of Joanna played across her mind. My God, she thought. My God.

CHAPTER 5

If she caught the lights just right, Karen knew, she'd have time to pick up doughnuts to go with the morning's coffee. Moonlight fell across the lawns and rooftops, highlighting familiar objects in a cold silver iridescence, adding a dreamlike quality to everything it touched. A dog barked somewhere in the distance, a sharp clear sound, slicing through early morning darkness and disappearing into the softening edges of night.

In only four weeks, Karen felt like a valued member of the patient-care team at the clinic. She spent every Monday and Wednesday morning assisting Joanna with surgical procedures, and was delighted to discover her old skills returning. Immersed again in her own medium, she could scarcely believe she had been away from nursing for fifteen years. With each new or reclaimed competence, Karen gained increasing confidence in herself, and with that confidence came a new sense of freedom and the growing belief that, if necessary, she could support herself and her sons.

Karen thoroughly enjoyed work at the clinic, especially the time spent in Joanna's company. The better she got to know Joanna, the more she liked her, and the two were used to getting away for lunch whenever possible. Karen looked forward to their meetings and guarded against interruptions.

The doughnut shop was almost empty, and in less than five minutes, Karen had purchased a box of twelve assorted honey-dipped, creme-filled, chocolate-frosted and old-fashioned doughnuts.

Ten minutes later, she pulled into the staff lot and parked next to Joanna's white Riviera. As Karen walked up the back porch stairs, Joanna opened the door and called out, "I thought I heard your car, I have a patient. I could use your help."

The adrenalin pumped through Karen's body as she ran up the remaining stairs and followed Joanna into one of the examining rooms. A small thin woman was lying on the table, holding an absorbent bandage on her forehead just below her hairline. Blood had soaked through the thick layers of cotton and gauze, and a thin trickle of blood trailed slowly down her cheek toward the corner of her ear.

Joanna held the woman's hand and spoke to her

47

comfortingly. "You're going to be fine, Maria. Your baby isn't hurt. I can hear a good strong heartbeat." She lifted the sterile pad and looked at the wound on Maria's head. "You're going to need some sutures." She looked at Karen. "I need one cc of Xylocaine and five-oh nylon."

Karen filled a syringe, prepared a suturing set, and placed it on an instrument table near Joanna. She watched as Joanna injected the Xylocaine along the edges of the wound.

She has beautiful hands, Karen thought, holding her breath as Joanna's hands moved slowly down the woman's cheek. Karen's heart raced as Joanna's fingertips brushed across the woman's lips with exquisite tenderness.

"I want to talk to your husband before you go home," Joanna said.

The words pulled Karen back to the present.

"If he ever hits you again, you need to have him arrested. You don't need to take any more chances with your baby."

"He says he's sorry," Maria said. "He drove me here, but he's afraid to come inside. He feels ashamed."

"He should feel ashamed." Joanna picked up the suturing needle and began to close the wound on Maria's forehead. "If he raises his hand to you again, you leave immediately." She tied the second suture. "If you can't leave, pick up whatever you can get your hands on and hit him in the head with it. The next time he's tempted to hit you, he'll think twice. And don't take his verbal abuse either. In some ways, it's more damaging than a punch."

My God, Karen thought. *Phillip's been doing that*

to me for years. I've had more verbal beatings than I could count.

A wave of nausea swept over her. How could she have taken it from him for so long? He was probably not much different from Maria's husband. Just a little more polished.

"We're almost finished," Joanna said. "One more."

Karen was touched by Joanna's obvious concern for Maria and her unborn child. She liked the sensitivity and gentleness that seemed so natural to this unassuming woman. No wonder her patients loved her.

She handed Joanna a fresh sterile pad, then the paper tape to hold it in place.

"Okay. You can get up," Joanna said. "I'll walk outside with you so I can talk to Tony." She looked at Karen. "I'll be right back. If you don't mind, maybe you could put a pot of coffee on. I sure could use a cup." She looked at her watch. "We have a D and C in forty minutes."

"Coffee and doughnuts coming up," Karen said. She was particularly aware of the vivid green of Joanna's eyes, particularly aware of the compelling attraction she was feeling. As she watched Joanna walk toward the front door, desire and fear filled her completely.

CHAPTER 6

The ringing of the phone pulled Joanna from a deep sleep. She reached for the receiver, then clicked on the lamp on the bedside table. Years of practice in obstetrics had taught her the art and necessity of moving from sleep to full wakefulness in a matter of seconds.

"Doctor Jordan," Joanna said softly.

"We're going to punish you for your crimes." The man's voice was harsh and deep. "Baby killing is punishable by death."

Joanna's heart leapt, her body preparing her for

battle. "Don't you people ever give up?" Months of frustration sent an avalanche of emotion crashing down on her.

"Not until we close every abortion clinic in this country, and get rid of butchers like you." His speech became slower and more deliberate. "You leave us no choice. If you won't stop what you're doing, we'll have to teach you. It's God's will."

Joanna was furious. "How dare you use God as an excuse for your violence. You ought to be in jail."

"Make your peace with God, Doctor. You don't have long to live." There was a loud click, followed by a dial tone.

"Bastard!" Joanna slammed the receiver onto its cradle.

"Another one of your fans?" Vicki's voice dripped with sarcasm as she pulled herself to a sitting position.

Joanna was in no mood to put up with hostile remarks. Her anger flared in response to the smirk on Vicki's face. "Don't start. I'm in no mood to get into another major argument with you."

"We wouldn't get into arguments if you'd get into a decent practice. I didn't sign on to be a target. If you choose to continue in this awful business, the least you can do is to keep it out of our home."

"How would you suggest I do that? I can't get an unlisted number." Joanna shrugged. "I'll check about getting an answering service in the morning."

"At this point, I don't care how you do it." Vicki's face was flushed. "I'm tired of getting the fallout from a cause I'm not really involved in. You figure it out."

"Do you want to sleep in the other bedroom so

51

you won't hear the phone if it rings?" In the past, she never would have thought of separate bedrooms as a way to quell Vicki's complaints about the clinic, but Joanna was tired of the litany.

Vicki looked stunned. "That's a solution? Rearrange our personal lives because you're not willing to rearrange your professional life?"

Joanna felt trapped. "I don't know what else to suggest. I don't want you to be unhappy, but I won't be scared off by a group of religious nuts."

Vicki's razor-sharp stare sent chills down Joanna's spine. Joanna decided to make one more plea. "If I had my way, you'd get involved in the pro-choice movement with me. Maybe if you felt a part of it, it wouldn't aggravate you the way it does now."

Vicki's eyes took on a glacial coldness. "I'm not sure if you're deliberately refusing to hear what I've been saying or if you truly have no idea of how serious this is." She turned toward Joanna. "I can't continue to live like this. I don't want to sacrifice my private life for a group of fanatics. I'm tired of having to do things alone because you're involved with the newsletter or out of town for some pro-choice rights meeting. If that's more important to you than our relationship, you should go for it." Her gaze held Joanna fast. "But we're getting to a point where you're going to have to make a choice. I can't and won't continue like this indefinitely."

"Are you giving me an ultimatum? You or the clinic?" Joanna's desire for conciliation had changed into anger. She hated ultimatums. The mere suggestion of being pushed into an either/or situation had always been repellent to her. More than once in the past, she had pulled the temple down around her head rather than give in to what she considered blackmail.

"I'm telling you how I feel," Vicki said. "I'd be happier if you didn't even have to consider which option you'd rather choose. It's not an ego-builder to realize that your lover would rather be off fighting for some cause than home sharing time with you."

"Why must I choose at all? Why can't I do both?" Joanna was frustrated, and nearing despair. "Come with me to Pittsburgh in the morning."

Vicki threw the covers back and got out of bed. "Not this trip, Joanna. I think you need some time to think, and so do I. We'll talk when you get back." She walked toward the door, coolly elegant in her silk pajamas. "I'm going to sleep in the other room. If I don't see you before you leave, have a good trip."

Joanna was alone. She stared at the door in disbelief. What was happening to them? She could feel them drifting further and further apart. She remembered a dream she had had two nights ago. She and Vicki were stranded on an ice floe, when suddenly the huge block of ice began to break apart. She lunged toward Vicki, but it was too late. They were caught in opposite currents; prisoners of an indifferent river.

She looked around the room, desperate to escape the isolation and loneliness the memory of the dream engendered in her. It was the same feeling that had tortured her following her mother's death, the same feeling made almost unbearable when her sister died.

Suddenly she was aware of the tick-tock of the bedside clock and the steady beat of her own heart.

They too seemed bound in different directions, point and counterpoint, demanding opposite commitments, splitting her in two and pulling her away from herself. She shivered as sweat formed a thin film against her skin. She struggled for a deep breath, but her own separateness saturated her consciousness and filled her with panic. Oh God, she thought, swallowing hard, fighting against the panic that would have her run in all directions. All she wanted was someone to hold onto, anyone, anything. Her throat was tight and dry as she forced herself to breathe more slowly, telling herself again and again, I'm all right, I'm all right.

She pushed the covers back and got to her feet. She would go after Vicki; she would quit the clinic. Her hand was on the doorknob when she gained control again. She leaned against the door and looked at the bed, trying to focus on something outside herself. She thought of Karen and her strength in facing Phillip, of Karen's courage in pursuing a nursing career after so many years away. The sharp jagged edges she'd felt inside faded and her breathing was no longer shallow. She climbed back under the covers, folded herself into their comfort, and slept.

CHAPTER 7

Joanna took a sip of coffee and tried again to concentrate on the position papers on the restaurant table in front of her. She read the same sentence for the third time before thoughts of Vicki and Karen overpowered her. It's no use, she finally admitted, my mind won't stay put right now. She shoved aside the menus the waitress had left with her ten minutes earlier and glanced at the large Coca-Cola wall clock that hung above the entrance. 6:25 am. Nancy should be here any minute.

She had met Nancy Cole at the same restaurant

every Tuesday morning for the past eleven years. It was a time the two could count on, no matter how frenzied the week was for either of them. Nancy had suggested the standing date when it became obvious that she and Vicki were not going to get along. It had been one more in a long line of compromises Joanna had made in order to keep peace at home, a long line that was looking more and more like a chain. How many more compromises could she make before the illusion collapsed under its own weight? For the first time in twelve years, Joanna was asking herself to consider the question seriously. She took another swallow from her cup and tried to think about the agenda for Pittsburgh. Her attempt fell easy prey to thoughts of last night's dream of Karen. The images were more vivid each time they entered her consciousness — her arms around Karen, the softness of Karen's mouth against her own, the warm curves of Karen's body beneath her hands. Ridiculous. Joanna dismissed the images. *Just because I dreamed about her doesn't mean I want to make love to her.* She took a deep breath. She felt wet and tight down below and knew that her body was more honest than her mind.

She glanced up to see Nancy walking toward her, her stocky, solid appearance oddly comforting to Joanna.

"Hi. I was afraid you'd overslept," Joanna said, relieved that she could pay attention to the here and now with Nancy.

"Why? I'm not late." She slid into the booth across from Joanna and waved to the waitress for coffee and the English muffin she always ordered.

"Were you at the hospital all night?" Nancy spoke with her usual bluntness. "You look awful."

"I didn't get much sleep. I had another threatening phone call around one, followed by an argument with Vicki." Joanna's honesty with Nancy was second nature.

"Just more of the same?" Nancy's brown eyes reflected her genuine interest.

"Pretty much. Vicki ended up sleeping in the other bedroom." Joanna paused. "I also had a dream that woke me up. I had a hard time getting back to sleep."

"A nightmare?"

"Not exactly, but it could turn into one." She watched Nancy's eyes for any hint of disapproval. "I dreamed about Karen Wainwright. About making love to her."

"You said she's very attractive." There was no sign of surprise or reproach on Nancy's face. "But if my memory serves me correctly, you told me she's married and has a couple of teenagers." Nancy spread strawberry preserves on the toasted English muffin the waitress had served, took a bite and washed it down with coffee. "As much as I think you need to get away from Vicki, I don't think getting involved with a married woman would help you one bit. In fact, to use your own words, it could be a real nightmare."

"There isn't the remotest chance of that happening." Joanna was answering herself as much as she was informing Nancy. "There's never been one word between us that's even remotely related to the subject."

"Then what's the problem?" Nancy asked.

Joanna shook her head. "I don't know, maybe I'm just being silly. I was surprised I'd dreamed about making love to her. I don't usually dream about people I work with." She played with her spoon as she spoke. "And I'd rather not feel sexually aroused when I think about her. It's a little unsettling."

"Oh." Nancy shook her head knowingly. "You didn't tell me that part before. Does this happen often?"

"Not really." Surprised at her own defensiveness, Joanna said more honestly, "Often enough. I just hadn't thought about it until now."

"Do you think it could be mutual?"

"Not at all. In fact, I think she'd be horrified if she knew I even thought about her in that way. After all, this is a woman who until a couple of months ago didn't go anywhere without her husband's approval." Joanna shrugged. "Besides, I have enough problems trying to figure out what I should do about my relationship with Vicki. I'd like to be able to make some kind of decision when I get back on Sunday."

"That's easy. Get the hell away from her. Split up what you can, take your losses on what you can't, and start a new life." She raised an eyebrow. "Not with a married woman, however, unless you want more problems."

"Listen, I'm not interested in any new relationship at this point. Maybe Vicki and I can work things out." Joanna smiled. "I'd better get going. My plane leaves at nine and I'm supposed to pick Karen up on the way."

"I wish she weren't going with you right now.

You're too vulnerable." Nancy reached across the table and held Joanna's hand. "You do have separate rooms, don't you?"

"Cynthia made the reservations. She knows not to put me in a room with somebody. Not that it would make that much difference." She was amused at Nancy's cautioning remarks. "I don't think either of us is in any danger of being seduced."

"You never know what other people are thinking, Joanna. You're much too nice to end up in the middle of a divorce." Nancy's tone was deadly serious.

Joanna laughed. "For God's sake, Nancy, I'm going to Pittsburgh on a business trip, not to Niagara Falls on a honeymoon. The schedule is so tight, I'll be lucky to get time to eat and sleep."

Nancy grinned. "Good. You won't have time to get into trouble."

Joanna remembered her dream of Karen, the taste of Karen's kiss.

CHAPTER 8

Karen followed the bellman across the crowded hotel lobby to the front desk. She gave her name and Doctor Jordan's to the desk clerk and scanned the crowd for Joanna. She spotted her just inside the front door still talking with the two women who had embraced her as she left the taxi. Karen studied the two women more carefully as she waited for their room keys. The tall redhead, Susan Crane, seemed warm and friendly when Joanna had introduced her to Karen. She didn't seem the type

Karen imagined on the front lines of a pro-choice rally. Much too ordinary to fit into her idea of a picket line for women's rights. The darker, older woman Joanna had introduced as Sister Mary Elizabeth Kyle. What would a Catholic nun be doing in a pro-choice movement? Karen pictured her in front of a seventh grade class, or leading a young people's choir, and thought how much more appropriate those activities seemed to her.

"I'm afraid we have a slight problem, Ms. Wainwright." The desk clerk's voice drew Karen's attention from Joanna and her friends. "Somehow the reservations were confused. You and Doctor Jordan are in the same room." He smiled. "I hope that won't be inconvenient. There are two double beds in the room."

Karen felt her heartbeat quicken. "I would prefer a single room."

The desk clerk scanned his computer terminal. "I'm afraid that's impossible. We're completely full." He placed two keys on the counter.

"You must have something." Karen felt her discomfort growing. "Size doesn't matter."

"I'm afraid not. Not even a closet. The Dental Association has booked everything." His smile faded. "I could try another hotel for you if you'd like."

Karen was afraid her apprehension was showing. "That won't be necessary . . . I'm sure the one room will be fine."

The clerk looked slightly relieved. "I'll send your luggage right up." He handed one key to Karen and one to the bellman.

"Thank you," Karen said. She decided to stop by

the newsstand and was walking in that direction when Joanna and her two friends caught up with her.

"We've decided to get lunch," Joanna said. "We can see our rooms later if that's okay with you. Did you get the keys?"

"Key," Karen said, and held up the single key in her hand. "They mixed up the reservations. We're sharing a room."

Joanna shrugged. "Fine. Let's get something to eat."

"You'd better watch out for yourself, Karen," Sister Kyle said. "The last time I shared a room with Joanna, she kept me up till all hours insisting we could get more work done before we turned in for the night."

"She did the same thing to me a year ago," Susan Crane said. "If she won't let you go to bed, you can come sleep in my room."

"That won't be necessary." Joanna put her hand on Karen's shoulder. "I promise not to keep you up all night."

The butterflies in Karen's stomach fluttered wildly. Joanna's green eyes looked warm and inviting. Karen was conscious of the weight of Joanna's hand on her shoulder.

"Don't believe her, Karen," Sister Kyle said. "She promised me the same thing."

Joanna put her arm around Karen. "Don't listen to them. I'm not half as bad as they make me sound."

Karen looked directly into Joanna's eyes. Danger and excitement were mixed in their depths. Karen felt drawn to both. "I'll take my chances," she said.

"Another innocent bites the dust," Susan Crane said. "And if I don't bite into a sandwich soon, I'm going to die of hunger."

"Let's eat." Sister Kyle smiled at Karen. "But don't say you weren't warned."

The white terry cloth robe felt soft and warm on Karen's bare skin. She towel-dried her wet hair as she walked from the bathroom into the hotel bedroom. Her short damp hair fell naturally into place, and as she draped the towel around her neck, she sat down on the corner of the bed and looked across at Joanna. The light green collar of her bathrobe almost matched her eyes. A notebook lay open across her knees and several sheets of paper and a magazine article lay on the bed to her right. Karen watched Joanna in silence for several minutes, noting the total concentration she was giving to the work before her. Excitement grew in the pit of her stomach, but when she felt a tightness between her thighs, Karen was annoyed with herself. This is ridiculous, she thought. I'm not attracted to women.

The tightness grew more pronounced, and Karen made a conscious decision to banish any such feelings or thoughts. She persuaded herself to think of the day's activities. There had been several hours of meetings after lunch, followed by a working dinner in the hotel. It was almost ten o'clock when several people decided they were too tired to continue. Karen had welcomed the declaration and was glad to see that the committee was well able to deal with Joanna's compulsive work behavior. They simply called for a vote and adjourned until 9:00 a.m. the following morning.

Karen lay back on her bed, intending to close her eyes for a moment before she dried her hair, put on her pajamas, and turned in for the night. Images of Joanna passed through her mind as she drifted into sleep. Without warning, Joanna's face was close to hers. She could feel the warmth of Joanna's breath against her cheek, the warmth of Joanna's body as she leaned toward her. Karen's mind was a battlefield of conflicting emotions and desires. Part of her wanted to throw her arms around Joanna, to pull her close, to cover her mouth with her own, to know the warmth of Joanna's kiss, her caress. That desire fought valiantly against the voice that bade her run and hide, that cursed her desire. Her body no longer responded to those commands. She lay in Joanna's arms unable to move, unable to want anything except Joanna. The thought, the emotion, the hunger, filled her so completely that she could feel Joanna's presence in the very essence of herself. Joanna and she were one! Joanna's kiss flowed through her veins, pulsed against her temples, beat hard against her chest. She inhaled deeply, drawing Joanna into herself, filling herself with this otherness, becoming what they were together, losing all that was not born of them. Pleasure rose up inside her, claimed her for its own, set her drifting in itself. The echoes of her own desire filled her ears and her body moved like wheat caressed by a gentle breeze. It flowed beneath Joanna, matching her presence inch for inch, electrified with fulfillment.

Something was pulling her away. A loud, harsh sound, demanding her attention. She fought to close it out, to concentrate on the sum of what they were together, to turn away from all that was not them.

"Karen." Her name crashed against her ears. "Karen." She opened her eyes and saw Joanna looking down at her. She was filled with a desire to put her arms around her and hold her close. She reached up and ran her fingertips lightly along Joanna's cheek. The skin felt soft and smooth beneath her hand.

Joanna's hand closed around Karen's and held it still. "Karen, are you all right? You called out in your sleep. Were you having a bad dream?"

The question triggered Karen's memory, and once again she felt Joanna's mouth against her own.

"What is it? You're so pale." Joanna sat down on the bed next to Karen and reached for her pulse.

Karen was beginning to feel embarrassed. "I'm fine, Joanna. It was just a dream." She was drawn to Joanna's eyes and all the mysteries that lay waiting there.

The phone rang.

Joanna reached across Karen. "Hello." Her voice sounded distant. "Of course I'm here. Where did you think I'd be?"

Karen watched Joanna intently.

"You know perfectly well that I'll be home Sunday evening!" Joanna was distinctly annoyed. "If you're that lonely, ask one of your friends to stay with you a few days." Joanna's face had turned medium red. "That's not exactly true. I asked you to come with me and you said no."

Karen was acutely aware of Joanna's body. She stared at the V-shaped gap at the top of the green robe. The angle of her vision revealed the soft curve of Joanna's breast. Without a doubt, the warm wetness between her thighs was the direct result of the attraction she felt toward this woman. Her eyes continued downward, mesmerized, stopping on the bare skin of Joanna's thighs and following their nakedness upward to the point where the folds of Joanna's robe touched again.

"We'll talk about this when I get home." Joanna's voice sounded far away, flat.

My God, Karen thought, I'm as turned on as I've ever been with a man. I can't believe this. What's wrong with me?

"Good night, Vicki."

Joanna hung up and turned toward her. She couldn't take her eyes off Joanna's mouth, its shape, its color, the hint of moistness along her bottom lip. Karen was obsessed with images: Joanna leaning toward her, the sensual touch of Joanna's lips, the warm wetness of her mouth.

"You're still as white as a sheet," Joanna said. She reached again for Karen's pulse. "Are you sure you're all right?"

Before Karen had time to think, she was speaking her thoughts. "Are you still in love with Vicki?"

The blood drained from Joanna's face. She didn't answer.

"I don't think you are, but I can't always tell."

"I'm surprised you'd ask me that question." Joanna looked stunned.

"I'm sorry. Maybe I shouldn't have." Karen couldn't shake her desire to wrap her arms around Joanna, to feel Joanna's heartbeat against her breast, to feel Joanna's mouth against her own. "If I'm wrong, I apologize, but I don't think I am."

Karen felt Joanna withdraw. "Why do you want to know?"

Don't stop now, Karen told herself. You've gone too far. Be honest with her.

"I've dreamed about you several times," Karen said. "I was dreaming about you tonight when you woke me up." Karen kept her eyes focused on Joanna's. "I dreamed I was kissing you — that we were making love." Her heart thudded, and she could hear the rhythm inside her head. Her throat was closing, the dryness suffocating her words. She swallowed hard. "I wanted you very much." Her voice seemed to come from outside herself. She closed her eyes and inhaled deeply. Warm tears slipped slowly down her cheeks. "God, Joanna." She looked directly into Joanna's eyes. "I still want you. I want to feel your body against mine. I want to feel your mouth on mine." She paused to swallow the tears she was fighting. "I don't know how it happened, but I think I'm . . . I'm . . ." She covered her mouth with her hand, not wanting to say or hear the rest of her thoughts, the rest of her feelings. Her throat ached, and she knew she was close to losing control. A sob escaped her throat, then another, and another. Her body was shaking now. Oh God, she thought, it's too late to take it back.

She never saw Joanna move toward her. Suddenly, Joanna's arms were around her, and her cheek was against Joanna's face.

"It's all right, Karen." Joanna's voice was comforting. "It's all right."

Joanna's hand caressed her face, wiping her tears away. Karen caught her breath as Joanna brushed her lips lightly against her own. She felt her body tighten as pleasure flowed through her. Joanna's mouth covered hers; the tender firmness of Joanna's lips and the gentle nudging of Joanna's tongue struck a fire in the depths of Karen's being, set her spinning in a world of desire — a world where feeling reigned supreme. Joanna's tongue explored Karen's mouth, seducing the fire that lay hidden in Karen's soul. She pressed her body against the softness of Joanna and pulled her deeper inside her mouth. No longer a passive recipient, Karen covered her face with kisses.

How wonderful, she thought. How soft she is, how pliant, how gentle.

Joanna's hands caressed her body, down her back, upward along her waist, upward still to the curve of her breasts. She felt her body stiffen as desire flowed outward, sending rivers of pleasure cascading over her like warm water.

Joanna's body pressed against her, guiding her gently backwards until she lay cushioned against the bed. Joanna's hands moved quickly, untying Karen's robe and then her own. Cloth fell away and the satin softness of Joanna's skin warmed and melted Karen's body until she no longer knew where she ended and Joanna began. She pulled Joanna more firmly against her, opening her mouth wider, taking Joanna deeper inside herself.

Suddenly, a scream crashed through her, loud and shrill. Again, the awful sound, louder and shriller still.

Joanna's voice was insistent. "Don't answer it."

Her arms pulled Karen back. "Let it ring." It was too late. Karen had lifted the receiver.

Joanna's finger rested against her mouth. "Hang up," she whispered. "They'll think it was a wrong number."

"Mom?" Eric's voice fell into the room like ice. "Are you there, Mom?"

Karen pulled herself to a sitting position and took a deep breath. A thin layer of perspiration covered her skin; her heart was beating wildly. Joanna's eyes were green fire devouring her attempt at control.

"Mom," Eric called.

"I'm here, Eric." Karen fought to ignore her body.

"What took you so long?" Eric asked. "I thought I had the wrong room."

"I was sound asleep. It took me a minute to wake up."

Joanna moved away and Karen was aware of cold air against her skin. She pulled her robe closed and tied it around her.

"Dad's not here and Mrs. Driscal won't sign for me to go on a rock climbing field trip unless you or Dad says it's all right."

"What field trip, honey?" Karen tried to listen to Eric's words. "You didn't mention it to me before."

"It just came up. Everybody's going, so tell Mrs. Driscal I can go too."

There was a moment of silence, then Ammie Driscal's voice came over the receiver.

"Hi, Karen. I'm sorry to bother you, but Phillip is out of town until tomorrow evening, and Eric says

69

he has to return the release by tomorrow morning. Is it okay to let him go?" Ammie's voice delivered marriage and family in every syllable. "The school has four teachers going with them. It looks fine to me, but I wanted to check just in case."

"I didn't realize Phillip was going out of town," Karen said. "Are the boys staying with you?"

"Just until tomorrow evening. Believe it or not, they haven't given me one moment's trouble, aside from missing you. I think they were fine until Phillip had to leave too. Anyway, do you want me to sign this thing for Eric or not?"

"Sure, go ahead and sign it. He's gone with them before. They're very good about supervision."

"Well, that will make Eric happy," Ammie said. "How about you? How are you doing? No problems with the Doctor, I hope. You sure don't need that complication in your life."

What was it she had told Ammie? Something to the effect that she wasn't attracted to women, so it wouldn't matter if Joanna made a pass. It seemed ages since she had spoken those words. Ages and light years from where she sat now.

"Karen, are you listening to me?" Ammie's voice was louder. "Do you have company?"

"No." Karen wondered why she didn't just say, I'm sharing a room with Joanna. "I'm just tired."

"Well, I'll let you get to sleep," Ammie said. "I'm glad you're having a good time. A *normal* good time."

"Thanks for taking care of the kids," Karen said. "I'll buy you dinner when I get back."

Karen hung up and sat motionless for a moment. When she looked up, Joanna was watching her

70

intently. Concern had replaced the passion in her eyes.

"You look like someone who was just saved by the bell," Joanna said. "Is that what you're feeling?"

Karen felt embarrassed. The sensitivity she loved in Joanna didn't feel good at the moment.

"I wasn't expecting a phone call." Karen's discomfort was mounting. "I guess it's one of the hazards of being a mother."

Joanna didn't speak. Her eyes remained riveted on Karen.

"I didn't realize how tired I am. I'm afraid I'm about to fall asleep." Karen could feel the heat in her face, and she knew she was blushing at the insincerity she heard in her own voice. What must Joanna think of her? She didn't like herself much at the moment.

Joanna stood up, moved to her own bed, and sat down across from Karen.

"If I made you uncomfortable, Karen, I apologize. I should have realized you'd have second thoughts. I really wasn't trying to take advantage of you. I hope you believe that."

The desire she felt for Joanna, the passion her kisses ignited, the excitement she felt in her touch, were very real and very strong. So was the embarrassment she had felt when Ammie questioned her, and the guilt she had felt at the sound of Eric's voice.

"I never thought you were." Karen forced a half-hearted smile. "I was the one who chose to tell you what I was feeling. I'm not taking what I said back. I just need some time."

Joanna's expression was kind. "I understand. If

you want to talk about it at some point, let me know."

"I do have one question, if you don't mind." Karen's stomach felt like a butterfly ranch. "Are you and Vicki lovers?"

"We have been," Joanna said. "I'm not quite sure what we are now. Not lovers, not roommates, but not just friends either. I guess what has held us together is history." She smiled wearily. "The hold, however, seems to grow weaker every day."

Karen was touched by Joanna's sincerity. She felt a strong desire to hold her. With a gigantic effort of will, she suppressed her impulses.

"Thanks for being honest with me." She felt drawn by Joanna's mouth. "I may take you up on your offer to talk in the future. I'm just too tired at the moment."

"The offer stands," Joanna said. "Good night, Karen."

CHAPTER 9

When the wake-up call rang at 7:30 a.m., Joanna was surprised to find a note from Karen on the nightstand. Her first thought was that Karen had decided to return to Atlanta immediately.

I should never have kissed her, she thought as she read the note. She felt slightly relieved to learn that Karen had gone for a walk and would meet her in the coffee shop for breakfast.

She showered and dressed quickly, planning to apologize and assure Karen that it wouldn't happen again. In fact, she thought, I'll offer to move in with

Sue Crane. Maybe that will make her feel a little more comfortable.

She pushed the elevator button for the lobby. She really should have known better. She'd probably wrecked any chance of being friends with her. Joanna's anxiety level rose as the elevator descended. Would Karen leave the clinic?

For an instant Joanna wanted to forget the whole thing, to push the button for the 14th floor and act as if nothing had happened. Just as quickly, the thought was gone, and she was walking toward the coffee shop.

"I ordered you coffee," Karen said as Joanna sat down opposite her. "I'm glad you found my note. You were sound asleep when I left. "

Joanna wanted to run in all directions at once. She felt embarrassed and inadequate, and resented not being in control of her emotions. Emotions that were already rebelling against her firm resolve "not to let it happen again." Like it or not, she was definitely attracted to this woman. But it was more than attraction. She genuinely liked Karen Wainwright, enjoyed her company, looked forward to talking with her, and respected her intelligence and willingness to try new things.

"I was afraid you'd gone back to Atlanta." Joanna watched Karen closely, looking for any clue to what she was feeling. "I feel responsible for what happened and I owe you an apology." She looked directly into Karen's eyes. "I don't want to lose your friendship because of a stupid mistake. It won't happen again."

"I thought about leaving," Karen said, running her fingertips around the rim of her cup. "I decided that wouldn't solve the problem." She met Joanna's gaze. "What happened wasn't your fault. I was the one who brought the subject up." The briefest hint of a smile played at the corners of her mouth. "I think I know you well enough to know you would never have done or said anything to me, if I hadn't spoken first."

Joanna was touched by Karen's sensitivity and honesty. She took a swallow of coffee, wishing she could swallow her desires as easily. "You're very kind," she said. "But, I'm not sure you're entirely right." She knew she was taking a chance with Karen's friendship, but maybe they were already past the point of keeping it intact. Joanna felt her hands trembling, and for an instant considered changing the subject. No, she thought. This has gone too far to ignore. She inhaled deeply and drew her left hand into a loose fist. "Karen, sooner or later, I would have told you how I feel. My feelings for you didn't start last night, and they didn't stop last night either." She felt emotionally clumsy, stumbling over her words, falling into an emotional clearing where defenses disappeared. "I can't kid myself any longer, and I don't want to mislead you. I can't remember ever being more attracted to anyone." She felt the heat rising in her neck and cheeks. "I'm not talking about just physical attraction. I miss you when you're not around. I make mental notes about things I want to tell you. I see or hear something and I think of how you'd respond if you were with me." She rested her mouth against the back of her hand and studied Karen.

For almost thirty seconds, neither of them moved. Joanna felt frustration and defeat. "I can usually sense how someone is feeling, what they're thinking, but with you, it's like flying blind. I need you to say something. Anything. Just let me know you understand what I'm saying." Joanna wanted to reach out to Karen. She wrapped her hands around her coffee cup and waited.

"I've already told you how I feel." Karen's voice was low, almost inaudible. "I don't know what I was expecting from you. What I discovered about myself came as a shock. I knew I was attracted to you, but I didn't know how attracted until you kissed me. I didn't want you to stop. If Eric hadn't called, I don't think I would have stopped." She glanced down for a second. "Eric's voice brought reality back." She leaned toward Joanna. "The fact is, I have two teenage sons who need their mother. Two sons who would be devastated if they knew how I feel about you." She brushed a lone tear from the corner of her eye. "Because of them, nothing else can happen between us. No matter how much I want it to, it can't."

Joanna felt as if she had been punched in the stomach. There was no hope. No hope at all. I won't make it harder on her, Joanna thought.

"I understand." Joanna made every effort to keep her voice steady. "Maybe it would be better if I move in with Sue Crane after lunch."

"We have a meeting right after lunch."

"After the meeting then." Joanna was half hoping Karen would ask her not to move.

"I guess that would be best." Karen seemed saddened.

"I'll tell her you couldn't sleep with me working all night," Joanna said.

"Thank you. I appreciate that." Karen's smile was weak, almost half-hearted. "I guess we'd better go. The meeting starts in five minutes."

They stood up and Karen extended her hand. Joanna took Karen's hand.

"There's no reason that we can't still work together," Karen said.

"No." Joanna felt numb. "No reason at all."

CHAPTER 10

Karen had fought with herself all day. The pros and cons of her marriage passed through her mind like a long parade. Arguments for and against her friendship with Joanna interrupted the parade and scattered logic like so much dust, in all directions. Dry brittle thought was no match for what Karen was feeling.

The day had passed quickly, filled with committee business and formal politeness between Karen and Joanna. At lunch, Joanna had smiled when she stopped to tell Karen she would move into Sue's room immediately after dinner. There had been some friendly kidding about no one really wanting Joanna as a roommate, and Karen wondered at the inability of people to read the truth in her eyes, in her voice, in her glance. She didn't feel safely hidden. Quite the contrary, she suspected that her feelings and desires were like neon signs in a moonless night. She remembered what her grandmother had always told her as a child, "A guilty conscience needs no accusing." Was that why she felt so vulnerable? Was it her strong desire for Joanna that made her feel as if the whole world knew what she was feeling? Not even Joanna seemed aware of the depth of her desire, the electricity her presence sent through Karen.

Karen watched Joanna leave the room and walk toward the lobby elevators. She felt as if two indomitable forces were pulling her apart. Her head said, "Stay, let her go." Her heart wanted to run after her, to capture her again in her arms. There must be a place of compromise somewhere in between. If there was one word that summarized Karen's life, compromise was it. Dull, safe, life-losing compromise. She threw her napkin on the table and followed Joanna.

Karen used her key to open the door. Joanna was standing at the foot of her bed closing the top on her suitcase.

She turned toward Karen. "I'll be out of here in five minutes. I just have to get my things from the bathroom."

"I don't want you to move to another room," Karen said. Her body trembled as she spoke. "Please don't go."

Joanna looked stunned. She stood perfectly still, her eyes glued on Karen's face. "I thought we agreed that —"

Karen's heart was pounding against her chest. "We did agree, but I don't want you to go. I'm tired of always doing what everybody thinks I should. I've done that all my life, and all it has ever brought me is unhappiness. I'm tired of following other people's rules, and striving for other people's dreams. I don't want to live like that anymore."

Joanna, unmoving, looked almost like a statue. My God, Karen thought. Maybe she's changed her mind. Maybe she wants to move. She may as well know now.

"If you've changed your mind, I'll understand," Karen said. *Oh God, I hope you haven't changed your mind.*

"I'm not sure I understand what you're telling me," Joanna said. "I don't want to make another mistake and lose your friendship entirely."

Karen walked toward Joanna and ran her fingers along her cheek. The smooth warmth sent shivers up her spine. "I want to be more than a friend to you."

Joanna stepped back.

"What's wrong?" Karen felt rejected.

"I'm not sure you know what you're doing. Things aren't really different from yesterday. Your sons could call just as they did last night, and you'd feel guilty all over again."

"I've done a lot of thinking since last night." Karen picked up the phone. "Please don't put any calls through until nine in the morning," she instructed the desk. She replaced the receiver and leaned toward Joanna.

She held Joanna's face in her hands, kissed her eyes and her mouth. "I know neither one of us is in a perfect situation right now." Her hands shook slightly. "I know that neither of us knows how this may end, but I do know that I want to make love with you. I'm willing to take my chances. I hope you are too." She felt embarrassed. "I'm afraid I don't know how to make love to a woman."

Joanna was quiet. Had Karen made a mistake? Had she read too much into Joanna's behavior last night? Was it too late to save face?

Suddenly Joanna's arms were around her, and Joanna's lips were kissing her eyes, her forehead, her cheeks, her nose, her lips. It was as if someone had struck a match sending heat and light into Karen's blood, leaving brighter fires in their wake.

Joanna's tongue journeyed back and forth across her lips, pushing gently deeper into her mouth, finding her desire. She wrapped her arms more tightly around Joanna and pulled her closer. Her body was lighted by Joanna's touch, Joanna's body, Joanna's love.

On Joanna's bed, she lay burning with need as Joanna's mouth covered hers, Joanna's tongue probing every inch of the hot, wet darkness. She felt Joanna's fingers unbuttoning her blouse, pushing it back, reaching under her bra and pulling it away from her breasts.

Her own hands pulled Joanna's blouse free from her slacks, running her hands along the warm, smooth skin that lay beneath. Her fingertips found

Joanna's nipples and she squeezed them gently until they grew firm beneath her touch.

Joanna's mouth caressed her breasts, her tongue making small circles on her rock-hard nipples, squeezing them between her lips.

She caught her breath. Joanna's fingers inched down her stomach and sought the hungry passion between her thighs.

Her body was an electrified wave, music from Joanna's touch. With kisses and caresses, they undressed each other, tasting desire as they unwrapped the mystery that lay before them.

Karen sank her fingers into Joanna's hair. Joanna's fingers moved between her thighs, and Karen arched to meet her blazing touch. With each stroke, the flames leapt higher and then suddenly, gently, Joanna was deep inside her. Karen sighed as she surrendered to her, wanting her deeper and deeper.

Karen gasped as pleasure lifted her higher. Joanna's kisses moved downward, between Karen's thighs. Waves of delight washed over her as Joanna's tongue ran along the soft, hot lips, and touched the firm jewel.

Karen closed her eyes and floated in the waves of ecstasy that began deep inside her, enveloping her completely, carrying her in their power, transforming her into intimacy unhoped for, pleasure undreamed of. It seemed to last forever, hot, electric, and unbelievably intense. Then, in an instant, it broke, scattering Karen like ten thousand burning lights across a field of velvet black.

Even now, Joanna did not stop. Her fingers pushed, her tongue stroked, and Karen's lips swelled again, her rigid pearl straining toward an intensity she had not imagined before now. Arching upward, she exploded into ultimate pleasure and fulfillment.

She was floating now, free of all constraints, touched only by Joanna's love, free within the circle of her arms. Joanna enclosed her with kisses sweet and gentle. Karen ran her hands along Joanna's back, delighting in the smooth skin and soft curves that fit her perfectly. Her hands cupped the roundness of Joanna's hips.

Joanna kissed her eyes, brushing her lips across her lashes, her mouth claiming Karen with her gentleness.

Karen's hands brushed Joanna's inner thighs, moved upward and brushed the swollen softness between Joanna's legs.

"I want to make love to you," Karen whispered. "I want to make you feel as good as you've made me feel." She kissed Joanna deeply and covered Joanna's body with her own. Her heart pounded as her hands explored Joanna's skin. Her excitement increased as she felt the firmness of Joanna's nipples against her palms. Joanna sighed and moved under her, pulling Karen closer to her. Karen was on fire with desire. Her mouth trailed kisses along Joanna's neck and shoulders, until she found Joanna's erect nipples. Karen's tongue drew hot, wet circles, her lips encircled them, their firmness was hard against her tongue, their fullness supple in her mouth. How wonderful, Karen thought. How unlike a man. She let her fingers brush the texture of her hair, trace the satiny smoothness of Joanna's inner thighs.

Karen could feel Joanna's fingers threaded through her hair, guiding her almost imperceptibly.

The thought of Joanna's desire inflamed Karen's passion. She caught her breath as she touched Joanna's warm wetness, her satin lips, and glided over the erect jewel, rolling it between her fingers, stroking it, listening to Joanna's soft moans of pleasure, delighting in the undulating movements of Joanna's body.

Karen moved slowly to the place Joanna had opened for her. She brushed her face against the softness between Joanna's thighs, tasting the sweetness that awaited. Joanna's sighs inflamed the passion burning furiously in Karen. She entered Joanna slowly, knowing the pleasure it would bring. Her mouth closed gently over Joanna's lips, and she held the pearl cushioned against her teeth, stroking it with her tongue, increasing her tempo to match Joanna's sighs. Suddenly, Joanna's voice rang in her ears, Joanna's body arched, and then grew rigid and still.

She lay fulfilled and warm in Joanna's arms, placing brief, light kisses on Joanna's eyes, her cheeks, her nose, her mouth.

She closed her arms tighter around Joanna. "I love you," she whispered.

Joanna held Karen. "I love you, Karen. You make me feel alive again."

Joanna lay awake listening to the sounds of Karen's breathing and remembering the softness of Karen's naked body against her own. Moonlight fell in uneven patterns across the room, holding Karen in a narrow band of pale, silver light.

Joanna ran her hand along the path of moonlight on Karen's hair and face, and leaned to kiss her forehead. How peaceful she looks, Joanna thought. For a time, she felt wrapped in the same soft cocoon, but then, as suddenly as it had surrounded her, peace disappeared like raindrops on arid land.

What would Karen feel when she woke up? Would she remember the love that brought her here, or would guilt put that memory to death? Joanna felt her muscles tighten at the thought. And if love was remembered, then what? Karen was bound by responsibilities. Joanna felt uncomfortable with her own questions. Even if they could manage regular trips out of town, and one or two evenings a week to be together, how long would it be before guilt and opposition from Phillip and her sons would wear down Karen's resolve? Not to mention the hell Vicki would raise if she had one shred of evidence on which to base her suspicions.

Nancy Cole was right, Joanna thought. It would be simpler if she fell in love with some unattached gay woman. She studied Karen's face. It was too late now. She was already in love with Karen Wainwright. The memory of Karen's kiss struck sparks inside her heart. The memory of Karen's nipples growing firm inside her mouth fanned the sparks into flames. Brushing her fingertips along the curve of Karen's ear, she felt a growing tightness between her thighs. *I've been attracted to her from the moment we met.* Joanna smiled.

Karen turned toward Joanna and threw her arms across Joanna's thighs. The warmth and weight sent chills through her, and she caught her breath, realizing how much she wanted to make love to

Karen again. She pushed herself down in the bed and lay on her side. She traced Karen's face with her fingertips, then kissed her gently.

"I love you," Karen whispered in a voice clouded with sleep.

Joanna wrapped her arms around Karen and pulled her close. Karen's skin was warm as their nipples touched, and she responded to Joanna's caress.

Joanna shivered as Karen's hand slid between her thighs and glided slowly upward.

"You feel so good," Karen murmured.

Joanna caught her breath as Karen's hand caressed the hot wetness of her desire. Waves of pleasure broke over her as Karen's fingers glided up and down along her swollen clitoris. Joanna's hands trembled as she cupped Karen's breasts and flicked her rigid nipples. She pressed her tongue against Karen's lips and trembled with delight as Karen's mouth opened and welcomed her inside.

It was as if the soft strains of Ravel's *Bolero* filled the room and seeped into Joanna's soul.

She kissed her way down Karen's body, pausing to give particular attention to her breasts, her navel, her abdomen, her thighs. She trailed warm, wet kisses along Karen's inner thighs, teasing the wet silkiness of Karen's lips, separating their folds, then devouring the sweet saltiness of Karen's love, inhaling the fragrance of Karen's desire. Joanna was electrified with longing.

Joanna's tongue danced faster and harder, sending wave after wave over them, until finally the ultimate crest, plunging them deep into pleasure's heart.

Joanna was filled to capacity with pleasure; filled to capacity with sharing; filled to capacity with love.

CHAPTER 11

"Would anyone like fresh coffee?" Karen asked as she glanced around the conference table. She made a conscious effort not to look at Joanna. She had completely forgotten Joanna's early breakfast meeting, and had been disappointed to find Joanna gone when she awakened, but looked forward to lunch alone with her.

Time dragged. At least she wasn't expected to take an active part in the meeting. Her mind refused to stay on anything except Joanna and last night. She was more sure than ever that she loved

Joanna, but not sure at all concerning the changes that love might bring. After all, she was legally married and the mother of two teenagers. Plus, Joanna was in a long-term relationship, and legal marriage or not, dividing the residue of many years could prove a difficult and painful task.

Karen chuckled to herself. *What am I going on about? No one has even suggested that Joanna and I change our living arrangements.*

She caught a glimpse of Joanna and felt a tightness between her thighs. There was no denying her attractiveness. And she was an excellent lover.

Joanna's voice sliced into her consciousness. "We'll reconvene at two o'clock. That should leave plenty of time for lunch wherever you choose."

"I still think you should come along to the Greek restaurant with us," Sister Kyle said.

"It sounds tempting, but Karen and I have some things that have to be finished by this afternoon," Joanna said. She put her arm around Karen's shoulder. "We'd better hurry. I asked the garage to have the car brought out front to save time."

For an instant, Karen wondered if she had forgotten an appointment with Joanna. No, she thought, remembering Joanna's note. She smiled. It had been a long time since anyone had gone to some trouble for the pleasure of her company. I like it, she thought. I could get spoiled very quickly.

The restaurant was crowded, but Joanna had reserved a quiet corner table. It was perfect for lovers. The waiter took their orders and disappeared.

Joanna looked at Karen and fought a strong desire to kiss her.

"I missed you at breakfast this morning," Joanna said. She watched Karen closely, wanting to learn everything about her. "I'm sorry I had to leave before you were awake."

Karen smiled, then blushed. "I was glad you left me a note." Her face was a medium shade of red as she looked away from Joanna.

Joanna was puzzled. It wasn't like Karen to be shy. "Is something wrong?"

Karen met Joanna's gaze. "I think I'm a little embarrassed by my own thoughts."

Joanna wanted more information. She couldn't afford bad judgment in what could be a crucial situation. "Which way is that? Are you having second thoughts?"

"I've had second thoughts about us for months." Karen's smile quickly disappeared. "I'm used to second thoughts. They're not comfortable, but they're not alien to me."

Joanna braced herself for what she feared would come next. Nancy tried to warn me, she thought. I should have listened.

For several seconds, Karen was silent. Then, as if she had reached some pivotal decision, she folded her hands in front of her and looked directly into Joanna's eyes.

In an instant, Joanna recognized the look. It was total vulnerability. For whatever reason, Karen had dropped all her defenses. Joanna waited with patience, and awe.

"I'm not used to feeling this way about a woman." Karen spoke just above a whisper. "I feel such passion for you, Joanna." She ran her tongue over her lips. "I know that's not exactly news to you, but what happened last night was something I didn't even have a category for." Karen's face had turned a deep red. "I would never have guessed that I could be so turned on by anyone, let alone a woman." She took a breath. "I thoroughly enjoyed making love with you. I didn't know what the hell I was doing, but it didn't seem to matter. No matter where I touched . . . no matter where *you* touched me . . . it was perfect. I can't even begin to describe the pleasure you gave me." The shade of red deepened slightly. "And, I can't describe the pleasure I received when I made love to you." She paused. "I didn't say that right. I meant to say, when I touched you. I was making love to you from the moment we kissed, but I had no idea that touching you, feeling you next to me, feeling you beneath my fingers, tasting you on my tongue, caressing you . . ."

For a moment Karen stopped talking and Joanna saw within her eyes all she had hoped to find. She trembled slightly as the power of Karen's words washed over her.

Karen continued as if she had never paused. "That giving you pleasure could bring such pleasure to me. When I woke up this morning, I wanted to make love with you again. I was sorry you were gone."

Joanna's excitement bloomed within her. Her desire to hold Karen was so strong that she was halfway to her feet before she remembered where they were. She sat down on the edge of her chair and caught herself on the corner of the table as her chair tipped forward.

"Are you all right?" Karen asked. "You're not hurt, are you?"

Joanna felt like a teenager, all feet and careening feelings. She took a deep breath. "I'm fine. Nothing's sprained or broken." She took a sip of water, trying to regain her dignity.

"I think I actually managed to shock you," Karen said. She looked like a Cheshire cat.

"Surprise is closer to the truth," Joanna said. "A very pleasant surprise."

"I think I've surprised myself more," Karen said. "I have a lot of conflicting feelings, Joanna. And I'm terribly uncomfortable with my feelings. I want to make love with you again, and I'm scared to death that it shows, that someone will look at me and see my feelings in my eyes. That someone will know my feelings aren't normal. I don't want to be such a coward, so wishy-washy, but I can't seem to help myself. It feels *strange* to feel this way about a woman."

Joanna wanted to be understanding — she also wanted to run. She didn't need these problems. If she was smart, she'd wish her luck and say goodbye. If she was smart, she wouldn't be in love with her.

"Despite all that," Karen said, almost apologetic, "I want to make love with you again. I know that doesn't make sense, Joanna, but it's how I feel. I don't know what I'll think or how I'll feel when I get back to Atlanta tomorrow, but here, today, I love you, and want you passionately."

Thoughts crisscrossed Joanna's mind like comets, leaving only shadows of light. Illumination rose from her heart. Love's fire and passion's courage marked her path. She wanted desperately to take Karen in her arms, to hold her close, to make love to her.

"Thank you for being so honest with me." Joanna struggled to keep a conversational tone. "I realize that returning to Atlanta may change everything. Part of me wants to say, 'Let's not go back,' but I know that wouldn't solve anything. You'd still feel torn, and I still have a relationship and a medical practice to resolve. I don't think either of us can promise a future at this point." She leaned forward. "And that's okay for now. We'll have to take one day at a time and see where it leads." She looked at her watch. "Right now, we have to get back to the hotel."

"Maybe we can go to dinner alone tonight," Karen said. "It would be nice to have that time together."

Joanna was glad that Karen wanted time with her. "Consider it a date," she said.

CHAPTER 12

Joanna took a sip of wine and watched the shadows of light from the fire dance against Karen's face. Everything was just as she had planned. The suite was large, with a fieldstone fireplace and a bedroom loft that overlooked and complemented the main room. A large alpaca rug filled the space between the hearth, the long leather sofa that faced the fireplace, and two floor-to-ceiling windows. The downy blackness of the rug stood in stark contrast to the creamy whiteness of the sofa.

Joanna had requested several tapes of big band

music and jazz. A mournful melody seemed to float downward, filling the room with its mellow sounds.

"You were awfully sweet to do all this," Karen said. "I wasn't expecting room service, music and a roaring fire."

Joanna leaned across the table toward her. "I wanted our last night here to be special."

"You've already made it very special." Karen put her hand over Joanna's. "Would you mind if we sat in front of the fire for a while?"

"I'd like that." Joanna pushed the room service cart to one side. She watched as Karen gazed into the flames. The dark skirt and sweater accentuated the shapeliness of Karen's body. Joanna followed every curve with her eyes. She could feel the smoothness of Karen's skin against her own, the way it had felt last night — cool, then warm, then hot. She wanted to feel Karen against her now.

Karen turned and met Joanna's eyes. "Do you know this song? It always reminds me of you."

Joanna nodded.

"Sometimes I feel so strongly that I've known you for ages," Karen said. "Your smile, your voice, the touch of your hand. It all seems so familiar." She touched Joanna's cheek. "Then it slips away before I can remember the scenes as I *know* they happened — before I can remember where or when."

Joanna put her arms around Karen and kissed her. She felt thrilled as Karen's tongue met her own and matched its passion. She began to dance slowly and Karen followed every lead. Joanna nuzzled her cheek against Karen's. "Somehow at this moment, where or when doesn't matter as much as the here and now." Her lips found Karen's ear. "But I know exactly what you mean. I knew what it would be like to kiss you almost from the day we met. What you feel like in my arms, what it would be like to make love with you. I've dreamed about it a thousand times, and I know we must have loved each other a thousand times before this lifetime, and will love each other a thousand times again. No matter where . . . no matter when."

Karen's eyes flashed with passion. She kissed Joanna.

Karen's tongue felt soft and warm against her own. It yielded willingly as Joanna pushed gently forward.

Joanna moved her hands slowly down Karen's body, burning its memory into her mind, a fiery brand melting past and present until they floated as one.

Joanna trembled as her hands lifted Karen's skirt, slipped beneath and touched the warm, smooth skin of Karen's thighs, the thin layer of cotton separating her from the passion that awaited her.

Karen shivered as Joanna's fingers slid beneath the thin cotton barrier and glided in the warm wetness that greeted her.

Karen pulled her closer. "I want you, Joanna." Karen's voice was husky with desire.

The words flowed over Joanna like fire over kindling. She guided Karen to the floor and lay beside her on the alpaca rug. Firelight fell across Karen's face, her eyes dark blue bottomless pools.

Joanna kissed her, then slipped her hand beneath Karen's sweater and the thin silk bra, and held Karen's nipple between her trembling fingers.

She moaned as the nipple hardened. She was

intoxicated with Karen, her senses alive with Karen's touch, Karen's taste, Karen's voice, Karen's passion. Memories of their lovemaking burned bright in her mind, fueled her passion.

With one graceful movement, Joanna removed Karen's sweater and bra. She cradled Karen's breast as firelight danced in golden shadows across her tawny skin.

Joanna bent forward over Karen's full breasts. Karen gasped as Joanna took her nipple into her mouth, covering it completely with her tongue. Shocks of excitement surged through her. Passion moved through her veins like liquid light. She undressed Karen hungrily, then slid her hand along her inner thigh.

More than anything in the world, she wanted to fill Karen with pleasure.

Her fingers moved in the hot wet silk, separating Karen's lips, circling the firmness of the pearl, moving slowly again along the silky lips, sliding slowly inside to the soft swollen folds. Her pulse quickened, and she closed her eyes and inhaled the light scent of musk. She ached, filled to overflowing with Karen and with pleasure, the tightness between her legs redoubling. She moved her fingers in quicker, firmer strokes along the swollen pearl, feeling its throbbing rhythm.

Karen was calling her name now. Deep and clear and undeniable. The sound kindled Joanna's passion, so that she hung on the edge of her own pleasure, pleasure so intense it filled every cell, so enduring it promised to last forever.

She felt the soft walls of the well close tightly around her fingers, hold her fast for an instant, then begin a rhythmic dance of pleasure, opening and closing like a flower.

Karen's groans became a low muffled sound as her body trembled. Spun from pleasure's edge and falling headlong into ecstasy, she and Karen were one again.

Suddenly, she was kissing Karen again, their bodies locked together.

"I love making love with you," Karen whispered. "I love how you make me feel, how my body responds to you."

Joanna pulled Karen closer. "I love you." She brushed her lips lightly against Karen's eyes. "I like making you feel good."

Karen smiled. "I love you, Joanna." She ran her fingertips lightly over Joanna's mouth. "I really love you."

CHAPTER 13

The closer the plane got to Atlanta, the more Karen worried about Joanna. There was no doubt that she had feelings for her, strong feelings, and that could be a gigantic problem in Atlanta. She'd have to be very careful now. Careful she didn't let her attraction to Joanna show. Careful that what she felt didn't show in her eyes or face when she looked at her.

"Would you like something to drink?"

Karen turned toward the flight attendant. "Coffee for me, with cream."

"I'll have the same," Joanna said, then turned to Karen. "You're awfully quiet. Would you like to talk about what's bothering you?"

She felt herself blush. "Does it show that much?"

"That depends on what you're asking about," Joanna said. "You don't look any different than the day we left for Pittsburgh." Joanna paused. "What shows is that there's something bothering you. If I had to guess, I'd bet you were concerned about where you and I go from here."

Karen felt exposed. She hadn't planned to discuss her fears with Joanna at this point. She wasn't sure herself what she felt about returning to Atlanta. She preferred to work out her fears and problems on her own before she talked them out with anyone else.

"I'm sure you're partly right." Karen smiled. She studied Joanna's face, wondering how she felt about this ambivalence. There was no hint in the clear eyes that met hers directly.

"I guess I'm feeling anxious about how I'll respond to my family and friends." Karen was paying close attention to her own words. "There will have to be some difference, simply because I'm different. I'm not the same person who flew out of Atlanta only days ago. I'm not sure I can go back to my previous life as if nothing has happened. I don't mean I want to move out and leave my family. I don't. At least I don't think that's what I want." She took a small sip of coffee. "I guess if I have my way, things will remain essentially the same for now. Except that I'll have a relationship with you." She took a deep breath as she felt the edges of fear creeping in again. "How I'm going to manage that remains to be seen. I know I want more time with you, and I also know Phillip won't like it."

Joanna showed the slight hint of a smile. "That's only one side of the equation. Vicki won't be crazy about it either."

"God, I hadn't even considered Vicki. I guess I think of you as single." She watched Joanna's face. "And you're not, are you?"

Joanna's expression was serious. "No, I'm not. I probably will be in the near future, but when, and even if, is still up for grabs."

Karen felt disappointed and relieved. "I guess I don't have to worry about time right now. It sounds as if we'll both have plenty to work out."

"First, we'll have to decide just what we're working toward. I'm not sure you can answer that question right now," Joanna said. "I'm not sure how accurate my answer would be at the moment." Her face softened and her eyes grew brighter. "I know I love you. I have no doubts about that." She put her hand over Karen's. "Where that love will lead remains an unknown."

Karen squeezed Joanna's hand. "I love you too, Joanna."

Joanna held Karen's hand and kissed her on the cheek. "Guarantees aren't worth very much anyway. I'm willing to take my chances."

Karen felt tender toward Joanna. She fought an urge to hug her. "We'll both take our chances."

CHAPTER 14

Joanna was surprised to find Vicki sitting in the den with three suitcases beside her chair.

"Are you going out of town on business?" Joanna asked. "I don't remember you mentioning a trip." She relaxed into a soft leather recliner across from Vicki. "Aren't you going to ask me how the meeting went? You usually want to know everything that went on."

Vicki's eyes were unrelenting. They impaled Joanna and fixed her firmly in their gaze. "I'm not going out of town," Vicki said dryly. "I'm moving out until you come to your senses and start treating me better."

Joanna was stunned. No matter how well she thought she knew Vicki, Vicki was always capable of an ambush. "Why? What brought this on? You weren't planning to move when I left."

"I had given it some thought." A hardness entered Vicki's eyes. "I tried to call you twice while you were in Pittsburgh."

"I never received a message." Joanna wondered what Vicki was up to. She knew from past experience that there was much more to come.

"I didn't leave a message. When the desk told me you weren't taking phone calls, I figured you were much too busy to be bothered."

"We had several crank calls," Joanna lied. "It was easier to stop them than to deal with them all night."

"How convenient. It's a shame though, that there's nowhere you can go to get away from your public." Vicki's voice dripped with sarcasm.

"Don't start that again." Joanna was tired of Vicki pushing her. "I told you I'd give serious thought to pulling out of the clinic and I will."

"Fine." Vicki's tone sounded final. "When you reach a decision, let me know. I've leased a condo on Lenox Road. I've written my address and phone number by the phone in the kitchen." She stood up, elegant in her silk shirt and pants. "If it's not too much trouble, would you help me take my bags to the car?"

"Just like that?" Joanna felt her anger growing.

"If I don't quit the clinic right now, you leave? How is this any different from blackmail?" The blood was pounding in Joanna's temples.

"It's hardly blackmail." Vicki's voice held little emotion. "One has to care about something passionately before it could be a source of blackmail. I don't think you've felt that strongly about me in a long time."

"We've had our problems, but I don't think your moving will do anything to solve them." Joanna's anger was rising. "You're acting like a spoiled child. You didn't get your way, so you're going to take your ball and go home." The muscles in her throat felt tight and strained. "Well, I'm tired of giving in to you every time you're unhappy about something. If you want to leave, then leave!"

Vicki didn't move. "You've got that backwards, haven't you?" Her voice was no longer calm. She braced her hands on her hips. "You rarely give an inch on anything. I'm the one who usually compromises. You're so used to getting your own way, you think anything else is punishment. You don't even realize how spoiled you are."

Suddenly Vicki's words sounded all too familiar. Joanna had heard them a hundred times before, and a hundred times before they made as little sense as they were making now. What's the use, Joanna thought. We'll never agree on this. We're right back to where we started. A sense of defeat settled into her. She was tired, empty, out of energy to fight, out of reasons to hope. She shrugged and shook her head.

"We just can't agree on this." Joanna couldn't argue anymore. "I'll help you with your bags."

Vicki looked shocked. For several seconds, neither of them moved. Then, Vicki was nodding and reaching for one of the suitcases. "Call me when you come to your senses." Her tone was confident.

"That works both ways." Joanna looked into Vicki's eyes as she spoke. "I hope we both learn something from this."

No one was home when Karen arrived. A note on the kitchen island said Phillip and the boys had gone to a ball game. It was signed "Eric."

At least somebody remembered I was coming home today, Karen thought as she carried her suitcase upstairs. She unpacked, put her clothes away, and sat down on the bed. The room seemed smaller and more dreary than she remembered. The sun-faded blotches on the dark green carpet and the drapes seemed more noticeable in the waning daylight. She ran her hand over a wrinkle in the light green bedspread. It too had lost much of its original color, beginning to fray in several places. A lot like our marriage, Karen thought.

She heard a car door slam, and went to the window in time to see Phillip and the boys, all of them wearing jogging suits, walking toward the kitchen door.

"Mom!" Eric's voice carried up the stairs. "Are you home?"

Karen started down the stairs. "I'm here," she called. Eric met her in the hallway with a strong hug.

"I'm glad you're home," Eric said. "Daddy's really bossy when you're not here."

As Karen entered the kitchen, Phillip kissed her on the cheek.

"Did you have a good time? I thought you might decide to stay over another day or two."

"Really?" Karen said in a matter-of-fact tone. "It never occurred to me to stay longer."

"I don't know why you had to go at all," Brad said. With his arms folded across his chest, he was clearly angry. "You left Daddy to take care of everything."

Karen felt as if she'd been slapped. "Brad, your father and I talked about my trip before I went. I also made special arrangements with Ammie Driscal to make sure you had everything you needed." She studied Brad's expression. "What made you think I was leaving Daddy with everything?"

A smirk slid across Brad's face. "Daddy said so." He looked at his father. "Isn't that right, Dad?"

I shouldn't be surprised, she thought. He's done this to me before. "Phillip, you didn't," she chided.

He glanced at her sheepishly. "I may have complained in a weak moment."

"Well, you never worried about me in that situation."

"You're supposed to do that stuff," Brad said. "You're a mother."

Karen was determined not to put her sons in the middle of an argument that was really between her and Phillip. "Brad, this is something your father and I need to talk about alone. I'd appreciate it if you and Eric went upstairs right now. You can get ready for school tomorrow."

"Why can't we stay?" Brad took a step toward his father. "Daddy doesn't mind."

"Mom wants us to go upstairs." Eric put his hand on Brad's arm. "Let's go."

Brad pulled his arm away. "Go yourself. I'm staying. She's not the boss, Dad is."

"Brad," Phillip said. "Do what your mother says. Go ahead."

"Okay." Brad sounded reluctant. "But I hope you don't give in just because she says she's sorry."

Phillip nudged Brad. "Go on now, son. Mom and I need to talk."

Karen watched in silence as her sons left the kitchen. Phillip, stroking his beard and watching her through a half grin, looked far too smug to suit her.

What's the use? she thought. No matter what I say, he isn't going to change. If change is what I want, I won't find it here.

"Don't be mad, honey," Phillip said. "He misinterprets things. He's just a kid."

Karen felt a strong desire to slap Phillip. "Did you tell them you had gotten stuck with everything?"

Phillip shifted in his chair. His lips started to move twice without a single sound. She waited.

"Not exactly. I don't remember." Phillip avoided Karen's eyes.

"You know very well that this is the first time I've gone anywhere by myself in years. It certainly didn't hurt you to play mother for a couple of days.

107

I've certainly played father to them often enough. I couldn't even guess the number of nights you weren't around."

"My nights away were for you and the boys. Any other woman would be glad to have a husband who works like a horse for his family." He leaned back in his chair and stroked his beard. "In case you haven't heard, society considers husbands like me a pretty good catch." He grinned slightly. "You always were out of step with society."

"That's a lie. You worked nights because you wanted to. Half the time you were supposed to be working you were sitting in some restaurant or bar with so-called clients."

"My work requires some entertaining. You know that."

"We both know your nights out involved more than clients and work," Karen retorted, resenting Phillip's evasiveness.

"You never had anything to worry about. My family always comes first." He leaned forward and ran his fingers along Karen's cheek. "It's nice to know you're jealous. But, you really have nothing to be jealous about. I'm happy with my marriage and my work, and I'm a lot better off than most of the men I know. Their wives complain they don't like sex, or they use it as a weapon." He reached for Karen's hand. "After seventeen years, I'm still attracted to you." His hand cupped Karen's breast.

His touch repulsed her. She reached up, moved his hand, and placed it on the table between them. "Don't, Phillip. I don't feel well."

"Hey, after being away for a few days, I thought you'd want to."

A wave of nausea swept over her. For several seconds, she thought she was going to be sick. "Phillip, you're not listening to me. I don't feel well. I don't think I could make love if my life depended on it."

Phillip looked like a disappointed child. "Did you take something so you'd feel better?"

"Yes," Karen lied. "But it hasn't had time to take effect yet."

"Wouldn't you just know you'd come back with some damned virus," he said, frustrated.

Karen was regaining control. If she could just get through the night without having to make love to Phillip, she could sort out her feelings and thoughts in the morning. "I'll take a shower, get some sleep. I'm sure I'll be fine tomorrow."

Phillip looked skeptical but resigned. "Well, you go ahead. I have to go by the office for about an hour anyway. I'll see you when I get back."

"If I'm asleep, please don't wake me," Karen said, hoping she wasn't pushing his limited patience.

Karen walked upstairs intent on a quick shower and a good night's sleep. She smiled as she thought of last night, remembering Joanna's arms around her, their strength, how safe she felt inside them.

The muffled ringing of a phone brought her back to the present. As she passed Brad's bedroom door, she could hear his words — "motorcycle" and "my father said he'd get it for me." She fought with herself for a moment. She'd tried to teach them to respect a person's right to privacy. She had no right to eavesdrop.

"My father says he'll take care of everything," she heard Brad say. "He can handle my mother. He's the real boss in the house."

Karen froze. Calm down, she told herself. Knowing Brad, the whole thing could be his wishful thinking. And yet, given Phillip's immaturity, the story could be true.

She stayed in the shower for a full fifteen minutes. The warm water slid across her skin, and she let the water break along the back of her neck and shoulders.

Suddenly Joanna was standing in front of her, arms outstretched, lips slightly parted, thin rivers of water winding down her body in shimmering silver.

Karen closed her eyes as Joanna held her tight and invited her kiss. Warm water sprayed down Karen's throat, Joanna's tongue was warm and wet, sending waves of longing through each cell of her body. Joanna's hands glided over Karen's skin, hydroplaning over curves, forming warm pools of sensuality wherever they lingered or stopped. Fast and smooth along the roundness of Karen's hips, slow and sensual as they nudged Karen's thighs and glided upward. They anchored on the satin fullness of Karen's lips, whirlpools rippling around the hidden pearl.

Karen's heart was racing now. She wanted to feel Joanna inside her. She held her breath as Joanna glided into the soft folds, plumbing her depths, pushing deeper and deeper.

She gasped. Kisses cascaded along her neck and breasts while Joanna's fingers stroked her tender places with increasing pressure. With each stroke, pleasure burst into ecstasy.

She called Joanna's name and it mingled with the soft patter of water. Pleasure rescued her, held her fast. She could almost feel the sun — warm, comforting, unending light that washed through her. "Joanna," she murmured, peacefully adrift, carrying the light with her, resting at last in the safety of Joanna's arms.

"Karen." The sound of her name startled her. "Karen, are you about finished?" Phillip's voice came from their bedroom. "If not, don't hurry. I'll join you as soon as I get my clothes off."

Karen opened her eyes and wiped her hand over her face. The shower was hitting the back of her neck, sending a fine mist against her face.

"Karen," Phillip called. There was a loud knock on the bathroom door. "Did you hear me?" He pushed the shower door open.

Karen looked at him, a knot in the pit of her stomach. "Phillip, I told you I don't feel well. I'm not in the mood, in the shower or out." She turned off the water and wrapped herself in the large green towel hanging near the door.

Phillip followed her into the bedroom. "You don't look sick. In fact, I could swear you were singing in there until I called you." He massaged her leg. "Maybe a little sex will make you feel better."

"Why don't you get me a ginger ale? Maybe it

111

will help my nausea." Phillip usually took no for an answer a lot easier when it seemed inevitable.

"Sure," he agreed apparently encouraged. "I'll get it right away. You just lie there and rest."

Quickly, she dressed in pajamas, ran hot water over a thermometer, stuck it in her mouth, and got into bed.

"Here you go," Phillip said, plunking her glass on the nightstand. "Fever?"

Karen handed him the thermometer. "I don't know. I'm kind of woozy. You read it."

Phillip issued a low whistle. "A hundred and two. I guess you really have a bug." He shook the thermometer. "Maybe I'd better sleep in the guest room. I can't afford to be out of work with the flu."

"Maybe that would be best for tonight." Karen put on one of her best forlorn expressions. "I'll miss you, but I don't want you to catch this."

When the door closed behind him, Karen breathed a sigh of relief. Phillip had always been a bit of a hypochondriac.

For years, it had been apparent to her that something was basically wrong with their relationship. Now, after knowing Joanna, the deficits looked more like bankruptcies.

She thought again of Joanna's arms around her, of Joanna's smile, her laugh, her kiss. She squirmed at the memories. She had never felt quite this way about Phillip. Excited, yes. Satisfied, sometimes. But loved? Rarely. In the beginning, but never after that. She felt used with Phillip, like a thing required for his pleasure, but *any* "thing" could have done just as well. It's not as if he's making love to me, Karen thought. It was more as if he was looking for relief, and she happened to be a well-worn habit he'd bought, paid for, and was always handy. She punched her pillow, fluffed it, and tried to stop thinking about him. She'd have to find a way out. She wanted to keep the boys and the house, but if Phillip wouldn't leave, and if she was awarded custody, the court would most likely award her the house.

She turned over on her side and thought about Joanna as she drifted into sleep.

Joanna stood at the top of the driveway and watched Vicki's car until it rounded a bend in the road and disappeared. Her gaze didn't waver, even when the car was long out of sight. She half-expected the car to reappear, to pull up in the driveway, and for Vicki to jump out and say the whole thing had been a joke. Ten minutes went by before Joanna admitted that Vicki didn't play practical jokes, and she rarely reconsidered a decision until it had played itself out to the fullest. Joanna always resented this aspect of Vicki's personality, hated the havoc it created when forces Vicki had never considered spun into motion and hurtled toward them.

She swallowed her panic and went inside to get herself a club soda. In the large fireplace across the living room, the black iron fingers of the grate clawed through a mound of cold, gray ashes. Joanna sipped from her glass and allowed the iced liquid to roll slowly down her throat. She felt cold and alone, cold and almost numb. So many years spilled into the past. All the surrendered hopes and smashed dreams piled one upon the other in a grotesque heap of possibilities, misused or never used, or worse yet, never even acknowledged. In the beginning, she had had so many hopes and dreams. Hopes for storybook closeness, hopes for communication so pure that nothing lay hidden from the other, hopes that together they would form an oasis in the midst of a lonely world. She'd dreamed that every day would bring them closer, that their desires, once clothed in the fabric of dreaming, would come true. Some had. Most had not. The record of success and failure had caused Joanna to doubt the value of dreaming at all. The thought left a bitter taste in her mouth and a hollow place in her heart.

She could go after Vicki and ask her to come back. It might take as little as a phone call. Depending on her whim, Vicki could be a benevolent dictator or an avenging angel whose duty it was to make life miserable for the errant, until they finally confessed their sins, real or imaginary. It then became Vicki's duty to see that the offender was never allowed to forget the offense. Contrition meant nothing unless it was accompanied by emotional suffering.

Maybe getting Vicki back wasn't the answer. It never had been in the past, so there was no reason to think it would be any different in the future.

She enjoyed Karen's company. If Karen could actually disentangle herself from her family, the two of them might be able to have a pretty good life together. Lord knows, Joanna thought, I'm attracted to her. She swallowed the last of the club soda and stared again at the mounds of gray ashes. She didn't

114

want an entanglement with someone who had no plans to leave her husband. And what about the kids? They were another unwelcome complication.

She refilled her glass, then threw a couple of logs on the grate. With the ashes shoveled into a bucket, she twisted the gas starter and struck a match. Blue flames shot up and enveloped the logs. She reset the fire screen and sat down again on the sofa.

Maybe the best thing to do was have an honest conversation with Karen, to tell her, "I don't want to play games," and that if she was only looking for a little excitement, she should count her out. She ran her hand through her hair. God, she sounded like a lovesick nut. She'd slept with the woman only a few times and already imagined her leaving her husband. A divorce would be stressful enough, but if her sons found out the details of her involvement . . .

Joanna didn't want to think about the what-ifs. She'd invite her to dinner, level with her, and find out what she had in mind.

She looked at the fireplace where the flames were multicolored now, dancing and surging upward. The heat of the fire on her face made her drowsy.

She'd invite Karen for dinner tomorrow, Joanna thought, and she drifted into sleep.

CHAPTER 15

After a shared supper — turkey sandwiches,
potato salad and pickles, Joanna relaxed at the large
oak kitchen table and studied Karen more closely.
Everything in her own body was moving faster,
beating harder, and waiting more expectantly.
Waiting for what? she asked herself. There was no
denying that she had very strong feelings for her.

"I missed you at the clinic today," Joanna said.

Karen's face lit up. "I'm glad. I missed you."

Joanna wanted to take Karen into her arms and

kiss her. Not yet, she told herself. She needed to have some idea of how Karen saw their relationship and her own marriage. She pushed her chair back and stood up. "I think I'll change my clothes and splash some water on my face."

"Don't take too long," Karen said. "I brought some dessert."

When Joanna returned, comfortable in pants and a sweater, she found a fire in the fireplace and, on the coffee table in front of the sofa, a plate of assorted cookies.

Karen handed her a glass. "Club soda with a twist of lime."

Joanna was impressed. "You have a good memory."

They clicked glasses. "To us," Karen said.

"To us." Joanna raised her glass. "In fact, 'us' is what I'd like to talk about."

"Really?" Karen said, joining her on the sofa.

"I'm not sure exactly how to put this, so if I seem clumsy with it, please be patient with me."

"All right. I think I can manage that," Karen said. "So talk."

"I think you know that what I feel for you is much, much more than friendship." Joanna looked into Karen's blue eyes. "I'm in love with you and I'd like us to have a future together." She took a deep breath and relaxed slightly. So far so good, she thought. "I'd like to know what you want."

Karen took Joanna's hand and held it between hers. "I love you very much. I want a future with you, too." She touched Joanna's hand to her lips and kissed her fingers. "But I can't just walk out on my kids. They won't be finished with high school for two years. I don't see how I could leave them before then."

Joanna was shocked. "What about Phillip? Does that mean you'll continue to live with him as his wife?"

Karen's expression changed completely to one of weariness and confusion. "Not if I can help it," Karen said. "I don't want him touching me at all. I just have to figure out what I'm going to do."

"Have you considered a divorce? You could still keep the kids," Joanna said.

"Not if he knew about us, I couldn't," Karen said. "He'd turn the kids against me just to get even."

"So you want to continue living with him until Brad and Eric graduate from high school?" Joanna felt disappointed and helpless.

"I don't *want* to, I just don't know what else to do at this point." Karen looked as if she were close to panic. "If Phillip knew, he could try to take the boys away from me." Karen wiped a tear from the corner of her eye. "I know I'll figure something out, but it will take some time." Karen kissed her lightly on the mouth. "If you love me, Joanna, you have to give me some time."

Joanna was filled with contradictory feelings. "I love you more than I could ever express in words," she said. "So much that I really want to share my life with you. I want to live with you." Without thinking, she added, "Would it be so bad if Phillip kept the boys?"

"Joanna, I want to divorce Phillip, not my children."

"I'm not sure I want to live with two teenagers."

118

"I guess it's difficult for you to understand what it means to have children. You've been on your own for a long time. Things aren't as simple when one has to consider two other human beings. I know Phillip can take care of himself, but Brad and Eric are only sixteen. They won't be seventeen for three months."

Joanna felt a wave of depression wash over her. Was she being insensitive? It was only natural that Karen wanted her children with her, but that didn't mean Joanna wanted them interposed between the two of them.

"Joanna, it will all work out all right," Karen said. "Just give it some time. Right now, I don't have a reason to sue Phillip for a divorce. Not a reason society would be sympathetic with anyway. He doesn't get drunk, he doesn't beat me, he doesn't neglect the kids, and he doesn't run around." Karen squeezed Joanna's hand. "If I had that kind of cause, I could ask for a divorce and get custody."

"He must have some flaw," Joanna said.

"Not that society recognizes." Karen sounded resigned. She put her hand on Joanna's cheek. "I'll get out as quickly as I can. I promise you that." Karen's eyes looked soft and warm. "I love you, Joanna. I want to be with you. But for now, can't we just put this aside and just enjoy our time together?" She smiled. "How about some music?"

"Okay," Joanna said. She saw no reason to continue the conversation at this point. She knew only too well that logic was no match for the emotion of a mother arguing for her sons. If she wanted a relationship with Karen, she'd also have to relate to her sons. At least, she'd have to try.

She pushed a button on the tape deck and the parade of cassettes she had chosen began to send their soft, romantic melodies into the room.

Karen was unquestionably beautiful. Her soft eyes reflected dancing flames as shadows moved like liquid gold across her face.

Joanna's heart pounded in her ears. God, I want to make love to her, she thought. She ran her fingers over Karen's cheek and tilted her head upward. The flames in Karen's eyes were like magnets pulling her forward. She bent slowly over Karen and brushed her lips against the softness of Karen's mouth. Her body tightened as Karen's tongue met her own and moved in a lover's dance.

Karen's body undulated in Joanna's embrace. She was tender and open as Joanna's tongue moved like an artist's brush that dripped passion with every stroke.

Excited, Joanna slipped her hand beneath Karen's sweater, beneath the soft silk bra, and brushed her palm against the firmness of Karen's nipples. Joanna felt light scratches across her back, feeding her hunger. She pulled Karen to her and kissed her deeply.

The room filled with music that fell against them like soft rain.

Joanna removed Karen's clothing, letting her sweater and skirt fall like flower petals in soft patterns on the floor.

When Karen tugged at Joanna's shirt, her fingers undoing several buttons, Joanna closed her hand around Karen's, stopping her. "Not yet. I want to make love to you first."

Karen relaxed against her, and Joanna began

with light feathery kisses that intensified as her mouth followed the curves of Karen's body. She knelt on the floor and kissed one foot then the next, trailing upward along Karen's legs. Karen's fingers were clasped loosely behind her back, and Joanna could feel her tender scrutiny. Joanna's hands were trembling as she reached behind to the fullness of Karen's hips and gently touched her secret, private place. Wanting her taste, she burrowed her tongue between the pink folds, skimming the swollen pearl, slaking her thirst with love and passion.

Karen thrust her hips forward, and Joanna lapped the pearl, sucking it gently then firmly, kneading Karen's fleshy hips in rhythm with her strokes. Cries of pleasure drowned out the crackling of the fire and the harmonies of "Endless Love." Karen's body quivered. "Don't stop, Joanna, don't stop." Suddenly, her body shook, then tensed.

Waves of delight crashed in Joanna as she reveled in Karen's ecstasy.

Karen's mouth felt hot on Joanna's. "I love making love with you, Joanna." Her strong fingers traced a line along Joanna's cheek. She pulled Joanna closer and kissed her again. "You make me feel so . . ."

"I love you." Joanna touched her lips to Karen's forehead. "I want to make you happy." She kissed Karen's eyelids. "I want to share my life with you, to fall to sleep with you at night, to wake up with you in the morning." Karen's eyes were clear, bright and completely without guile. "If you decide to leave

Phillip, I want you to consider living with me. There's so much I want to share with you."

Karen's eyes lost some of their liveliness. She ran her fingers along Joanna's lips. "Getting away from Phillip may not be easy. Not that he's in love with me; he isn't. He just hates change of any kind."

"Are you really planning to ask him for a divorce?" Joanna hoped she'd say yes.

"I have an appointment with an attorney on Wednesday. I want to keep the house so that Brad and Eric can grow up there. Phillip won't want to leave."

"You can stay here if you need to get away from him."

"Thank you. I may need to take you up on that." She looked at her watch. "Right now, I'd better get home."

"I wish you could stay." Joanna's candor surprised even her.

Karen kissed Joanna lightly. "I need to get home."

"Isn't tomorrow Phillip's day to take the boys out for dinner?"

"Yes." Karen sat up and was beginning to dress.

"Can you come for dinner again?" Joanna asked.

"I don't see why not. I could just come home with you after we finish at the clinic."

"Good," Joanna said. "I promise you something more than a sandwich."

"A sandwich would be fine," Karen said. "That way, we'll have more time to talk."

* * * * *

Joanna sat down at her round oak kitchen table and poured a mug of coffee for Nancy Cole and herself.

Nancy, wearing faded jeans and an even more faded red sweatshirt, stirred creamer into her coffee and leaned toward Joanna. "Well, I have a few questions for you. For openers, why did it take you three weeks to tell me Vicki had moved out? And second, I think I can figure out what happened in Pittsburgh, but for the record, I'd like to hear your version." She drank coffee and waited.

Joanna knew Nancy would be this direct. It was one of the things she liked about her, but the mere act of being so directly confronted always left her a little off-balance. "I think it took me this long to realize I wasn't imagining things. For the first ten days, I expected Vicki to be here when I got home. I could just hear her telling me I should have known she wasn't serious." Joanna took a deep breath. "I'm still surprised she hasn't changed her mind."

Nancy's broad shoulders moved in an infinitesimal shrug. "Has she been back since she moved out?" she asked. "It's not like Vicki to just walk off the field while anyone's still standing."

Joanna felt the faint touch of panic as she recognized the truth in Nancy's statement. It put her on alert again, trying to fathom the overall design in a situation that seemed on the surface all too simple. "I've asked myself a hundred times what she's planning," Joanna said. She felt helpless to define the situation further without more information. "I can't imagine what she's up to. She's only been in the house twice since she left. Both times during the day to pick up some clothes. She left a note each time saying she'd been here, and for what reason."

Joanna studied Nancy Cole's reaction. It was more than her silence, more than her rapt attention, more than the look on her face that seemed to say, "You can bet your assets you're missing something. Vicki Richardson is not the type to 'go gentle into that good night.' " She could almost hear the wheels turning in Nancy's head. Defensive, she raised her hands in a gesture of surrender. "Maybe she's not up to anything. Maybe she just wants to dissolve our relationship."

"And is that all right with you?" Nancy asked. "Are you willing to let the relationship go?"

"The relationship is already gone," Joanna said. "There's nothing to save. I've looked at it from every possible angle." She sighed. "God, I used to argue with her to save what we had, argue with her to make it better. It didn't work then, it wouldn't work now."

"This isn't like you, Joanna. You're much too calm, much too happy to be totally involved with the problem between you and Vicki. Which brings me back to my second question. What happened in Pittsburgh? Are you involved with Karen Wainwright, or someone else?"

Once again Joanna was thrown off guard by Nancy's forthrightness. She had planned to tell Nancy of her newfound happiness, of her love for Karen. She hadn't expected to be interrogated about Karen and her feelings. Strange, she thought. It made their conversation more of an inquisition than a celebration.

124

"You look pale," Nancy said. "Are you all right?"

Nancy's words seemed to come from far away, more an echo from the past than a voice from the present. Nancy's eyes were filled with concern.

"I'm fine," Joanna said. "It's just that I had planned to tell you about Karen in a very different way." Joanna felt cheated. "I wanted you to be happy for me, to celebrate my good fortune." Joanna reached out and took Nancy's hand in her own. "I love her, Nancy. I love her more than I would have believed possible." She squeezed Nancy's hand. "It's just as you said. Life has opened up again for me. The whole world looks different, filled with promise and possibilities."

Nancy's expression softened. "I'm glad you're happy, Joanna, but aren't you forgetting about Karen's husband and children? How do they fit into your new life?"

Joanna felt as if Nancy had punched her in the stomach. She resented Nancy's questions, her entire attitude. She resented having to deal with issues that complicated her life.

"Is she going to continue living with her husband?" Nancy asked.

"We haven't really talked about it very much." Joanna considered changing the subject, but decided against it. Maybe talking to Nancy would help. "It's not exactly my favorite subject."

"I can understand that, but it is something you need to take a good look at," Nancy said. "It might be a little crowded for you living with Karen and her family."

Joanna felt the depression that always settled on her when she thought of Karen at home with Phillip and their sons. "Karen wants to stay married until Brad and Eric graduate from high school. At least that's the way things stand now."

Crossing her arms, Nancy shook her head. "Joanna, how are you going to continue a relationship with a woman who's sleeping with her husband?"

"Sleeping with her husband" made Joanna feel sick. "We'll have to work something out about that. Karen doesn't want to sleep with Phillip any more than I want her to." Joanna pushed the thoughts out of her mind. "It's possible she'll change her mind and file for a divorce before then. She met with a lawyer."

"And if she wins, how are you going to like living with two teenagers?" Nancy sounded as if she already knew the answer.

"It isn't what I'd choose, but it would only be for a couple of years or so." Joanna didn't feel half as confident as she hoped she sounded.

"I love you, Joanna, but I can't see you living with teenagers. You're too used to doing what you want when you want." Nancy shook her head. "Teenagers will change your whole life. For one thing, you'll have to be extremely careful around them. If they suspect you and their mother are more than friends, they'll tell Phillip and anyone else who will listen."

Joanna hadn't considered that facet. The thought of it now hit her like a brick. She could feel the blood draining from her face.

"When Phillip found out, he'd probably ask the court to grant him full custody." Nancy's voice was deadly serious. "How do you think Karen would feel if the court took her kids away because of her involvement with you? Do you think your relationship could stand up under that kind of punishment?"

"I hope I'll never have to find out." Joanna tried not to let her devastation show.

"I hope you don't either, but you need to be aware of the possibilities," Nancy said. She poured herself another cup of coffee. "I don't want to beat a dead horse, but I think you should also consider that you don't know who Mr. Wainwright sleeps with besides his wife. You could end up with a lot more than you bargained for."

Anger was beginning to creep into Joanna's depression. "God, Nancy, you sound like the warning profile on an experimental drug. I don't want to hear any more." She pushed her cup aside. "I invited you to share something I was happy about, not read the riot act to me." She could feel the heat in her cheeks and knew her anger was visible. "I'm sorry I said anything to you." She leaned back quickly in her chair, her arm hit the teaspoon beside her and knocked it to the floor with a loud plunk. "Hell, I might as well have invited the Pope over and told him about Karen. He probably would have been less critical than you." She was fueled into fury. "I'm sorry I asked you to come by." Joanna stood up and began to pace. "I can't believe you're acting like this."

"Joanna, I'm not trying to be critical. You and I have been friends much too long not to tell the truth to each other." Nancy's voice was very calm. "I love you. I don't want to see you get hurt."

Joanna stopped pacing and looked at Nancy. Of

course Nancy isn't trying to hurt me, she thought. What hurts so much is the truth.

"Will you sit down and talk with me?" Nancy asked. "Or do you want me to leave?"

"I don't want you to leave," Joanna said. She sat down and took a deep breath. She could feel a growing tightness in her throat and realized how close she was to tears. "I . . ." She felt the warmth of tears on her cheek and struggled for more control as she wiped them away with her napkin. "I know what you're saying is for my benefit." She forced a brief smile. "But there's not much I can do now. I really love her, Nancy. And I really feel we're meant to be together. I feel as if I've been searching for Karen all my life — as if I entered this life to be with her."

Nancy's expression became one of resignation. "Here I am telling you how to secure the barn, and the horse has been gone for weeks." She leaned forward and brushed the tears from Joanna's cheeks. "Well, we'll both just have to hope for the best." She kissed Joanna on the forehead. "You deserve the best." She smiled. "No matter what happens, I'll be here for you."

Joanna felt surrounded by the warmth of Nancy's love and friendship. "Thanks. That helps a lot." She looked directly into Nancy's eyes. "I do understand what you're saying, and given the fact that I'm hopelessly in love with her, I'll be as careful as I can."

* * * * *

"The door's open, Ammie," Karen called from the kitchen. "You're in luck. I just made a pot of coffee."

"Thanks. I could use some." Ammie sat down and stirred sugar into her cup. "I was afraid I'd miss you. You leave awfully early these days."

"Well, you almost didn't catch me this morning. I have to leave in half an hour."

Ammie tugged at the sleeves of her Nike tennis shirt, then said abruptly, "People are talking about you and Doctor Strangelove."

Karen had expected this news from Ammie before now, but expecting it didn't ease its sting. She forced herself to look directly at Ammie. "What people?"

Ammie shrugged. "Well . . . neighbors, club women. You haven't exactly been hiding your relationship with her."

"Why should I?" Karen felt a mixture of fear and anger. "There's nothing wrong with our relationship."

Ammie raised an eyebrow. "Honey, she may not have hit on you yet, but the consensus of opinion is that Doctor Strangelove has her eye on you for her next victim."

Karen felt her anger growing. "I couldn't care less what a bunch of busybodies and gossips think."

"Well, maybe you should." Ammie's voice had taken on a vindictive tone. "I heard Phillip telling Carl he thought there was something unnatural about Joanna Jordan, and she damn well better stay away from his wife."

Karen's heart was pounding. "Phillip doesn't choose my friends, I do." She got up and took her cup to the sink. "I have to leave or I'll be late."

"Karen, you're not listening. Phillip is very serious. He told Carl if he thought you were interested in some dyke, he'd take the boys and divorce you." Ammie put her hand on Karen's arm. "He wasn't joking, Karen."

Karen panicked. She wanted to get out of the house, to get away from Ammie. "He has one hell of a nerve." Her cheeks burned.

Karen raised her voice. "My kids come first. I'm not involved with Joanna Jordan."

Ammie looked relieved. "I'm glad to hear that."

"I'm glad you're glad. Now, I have to leave or I'll be late." Karen held the door open for Ammie and followed her out.

"Where are you going?" Ammie asked.

"I have an appointment with my therapist." Karen slammed her car door. "I'll see you later."

"If you were smart, you'd stop that damned therapy and get back to making your husband happy," Ammie called.

If I were smart, Karen thought, I'd tell you to go to hell.

Fifteen minutes into her therapy session with Doctor Marcia Wade, Karen was still angry, and still hadn't broached the subject. She had started on the subject of special equipment the boys needed to attend a three-week program at a wilderness survival camp in Colorado, and finally switched to the subject of survival in general.

"I used to think people needed survival skills to give them a sense of confidence, in the unlikely event they were stranded in the wilderness without food or water," Karen said. "Now I'm not so sure. I think it's harder surviving in a suburban neighborhood where you don't expect things and people to be hostile." Her anger had sunken deep enough to push other issues to the surface. "I feel more and more as if I'm living in some kind of fantasy land where everyone smiles and says all the socially prescribed things to your face, when behind the scenes, they act like a pack of sharks hunting for the slightest scent of blood, so they can all close in for the kill." Karen didn't like the sound of her words and felt disgusted with herself. "God, I can't believe I'm saying this. I've never been paranoid before." She paused. "I feel like people are watching everything I do." Marcia Wade's blue eyes looked warm and safe. "What's happening to me, Marcia?"

"Why don't you tell me what happened to you this morning that made you angry."

Karen wondered if psychiatrists cultivated therapeutic voices or if Marcia sounded the same when she wasn't working. For the first time, Karen noticed that Marcia was a very attractive woman. She had an outdoor look that appealed to Karen. I wonder why I didn't see it before, Karen thought. Suddenly, she felt her eyes open wide as another thought surfaced. *Oh no! Don't tell me I'm going to start being attracted to women.* She felt herself blush from her neck to her cheeks.

"Something happened before you got here," Marcia said.

"I had a visit with my neighbor, Ammie." Karen could feel the anger returning as she thought about it. "She wanted to warn me that I and my relationship with Joanna — Doctor Strangelove, as Ammie called her — had become the chief topic of gossip at the Tennis Club and throughout the neighborhood." Karen clenched her fists. "It makes me furious that people I don't even know are discussing my sex life. How dare they do that. How dare they talk about Joanna as if she's some kind of freak."

"And how dare they put you in that category," Marcia said. Her words were like a knife, slicing through the barrier Karen had placed between her anger and herself.

"Damn right." Karen's voice shook with anger. "I'm married. I'm not even attracted to women." Then she faltered as she realized what she was saying. "Ammie has known me for years . . . I've played tennis with most of them . . . we've watched each other's kids . . ." Karen felt a heaviness descending on her. "How could they dismiss me so easily?" She felt the warm irregular pattern of teardrops on her face. "I thought they were my friends. I thought they liked me."

"I'm sure they'd still be your friends if you would get back with the program again," Marcia said.

"What do you mean?" Karen took several tissues from the box on the coffee table.

"Oh you know," Marcia's voice was very matter of fact. "Play more tennis, attend more meetings, have them over for coffee, see less of Joanna."

Karen could feel Marcia's eyes on her face. She waited for Marcia to say something else, but she didn't.

Marcia's words replayed in Karen's mind. *See less of Joanna.* She took a deep breath and let her shoulders relax. "I don't want to see less of Joanna. I want to spend more time with her. I just don't want to be the subject of their dirty minds or their gossip." Karen finally aired one of her worse fears: "I don't know how I'd deal with it if someone said something to my kids. I don't want them embarrassed, and I don't want them to look at their mother as if I'm some kind of freak."

"Do you think of yourself as a freak?" Marcia asked.

"No. What I feel for Joanna seems completely natural to me. I just wish everyone else wasn't so negative about the whole thing."

"I'm afraid there's not a lot any of us can do about society's attitudes, except live our lives as we see fit — despite what society thinks."

"Hey, if I had my way, I'd move in with Joanna today," Karen said. "But how can I? I have two teenagers to take care of. I don't think they'd understand if I divorced their father and moved them in with a woman they don't even know." Karen felt a sense of relief. "I think most people would understand my problem. There's no way I can leave before Brad and Eric graduate from high school. I'm stuck until then."

Marcia said calmly, "Is that what you want, Karen, to be stuck where you are for two or three more years?"

The question left Karen a little disconcerted. She struggled to regain her mental footing. "Of course not," she said. "But I can't just walk away from my responsibilities and commitments."

"That's true," Marcia said. "And I'm sure your responsibilities and commitments are the root cause for you staying where you are." Marcia's blue eyes held Karen. "I think it's more important that you recognize the primary reason you want to stay with your family."

"Which is?" Karen felt annoyed and a little frightened.

"I think you're afraid and unwilling to change your lifestyle at this point. You said it earlier. You don't want to be an outcast among people you consider your friends. Making a life with Joanna would mean major changes in most areas of your life. Friends, family, neighborhood, work place, not to mention the changes in roles you've become accustomed to. I doubt that Joanna is looking for a wife and a mother. You'll have to get used to being a lover, a partner and a friend. And I imagine some of your friends would be gay. So the way you would socialize would be different. They might attract more of the kind of comments and attention you don't like."

Karen's sense of relief was fleeing rapidly.

"In fact, you'd probably get a lot of comments and questions from your sons." Marcia stopped talking and watched Karen in silence.

The burning heat of Marcia's truth confronted her. Karen wanted to shove it all aside and return to the moment when it had not been spoken, when she had not heard it with her ears, but only feared it in her heart. She resented the message and the messenger.

"If that's true, I'll lose my children. They're too much like Phillip to understand anything. Even Eric. I couldn't tell them. Phillip has taught them a world of black and white, with no allowances for grays."

Karen felt trapped in the small shallow box society had constructed for her feelings. She saw reality rushing in like the dark waters of a raging river that had breached its banks and was charting a new course. Truth was threatening her life.

"I can't deal with this right now," Karen said. "I'm not ready to take on those kinds of challenges." She wanted the therapy session to be over. Marcia's blue eyes no longer looked safe. They had looked too deep and seen too much.

"Our time is up anyway," Marcia said. "Maybe by next week you'll be able to look at these things again."

Karen was anxious to get out of Marcia's office. "Maybe," she said, knowing that at this point she'd say almost anything to get away from Marcia and her truth.

CHAPTER 16

Karen arrived home to find Eric putting a suitcase in the trunk of Phillip's car.

"Hi Mom," he called as Karen got out of her car. "Dad's been trying to find you for the last forty minutes. He's upstairs packing."

Karen put her arm around Eric's shoulder and kissed him on the cheek. "What's up?" she asked. "Who's going out of town?"

"One of Dad's clients said we could use his cabin in North Carolina for the rest of the week. It's the same place we got to use last year." Eric's face and voice reflected his excitement. "There must be at least five lakes up there loaded with fish."

"How about school? You'll miss two days," Karen said.

"Dad talked to the principal. We don't have much on Thursday and Friday anyway."

Brad was standing in the kitchen unknotting the neck straps on two pairs of binoculars. He looked up briefly and continued what he was doing. "Dad's been looking for you," he said. "He even called the Women's Clinic. Doctor Jordan didn't have any idea where you were." He looked at Karen, his dark eyes narrowed. "He was really mad."

There was a loud thumping sound on the stairs and Phillip walked into the kitchen, tucking his sportshirt into his pants. "Did the boys tell you where we're going?" he said.

"Fishing in North Carolina," Karen said, glad that they were leaving for several days. "When will you be back?"

"Late Sunday afternoon," Phillip said. "I wasn't sure you'd be back before we left, so I left the address and phone number on the counter."

"I see Doctor Wade on Wednesdays," Karen said. "I've had the same appointment for almost a year now. Did you forget?"

"I don't keep tabs on you and your psychiatrist," Phillip said. "It's bad enough I have to pay for it."

This was an old routine, but Karen was determined not to fight with him. God forbid he should change his mind and not go out of town, Karen thought. With effort, she allowed Phillip's remark to pass without a comment. Anything to get him out of town for a while. Maybe if she had three or four days to herself, she could think more clearly about what she wanted.

"Anyway," Phillip went on, "if an emergency comes up that you can't handle, call me. Otherwise, we'll see you on Sunday afternoon." He ruffled Brad's curly dark hair. "Let's go, son. The fish are waiting on us." He glanced at Eric. "Get my fishing rod over there." He patted Eric's slender shoulders and looked at Karen. "It would be nice if you had sandwiches for us when we get home Sunday."

"All right. I'll make something," Karen said.

Phillip leaned forward and kissed Karen on the cheek. "See you later. We'll bring you lots of fish. Maybe we can put on a fish fry for some of the neighbors. We haven't had them over in a while."

Anxiety seized her. "That would be nice. You guys supply the fish and I'll do the cooking."

Phillip flashed one of his rare smiles. "Good." He kissed her again. "See you Sunday."

"Ms. Wainwright for you on line two," Cynthia announced.

"Thanks," Joanna said. She punched the button. "Hi, Karen, how are you doing?"

Karen's voice sounded strong and cheerful. "I'm doing pretty good. I was wondering if you'd like a house guest for a couple of nights?"

"Are you serious?"

"Phillip and the boys are on a fishing trip to

North Carolina until Sunday. Would you like some company tonight?"

"I'd love it," Joanna said. "Just use your key and make yourself at home. I'll get there as soon as I can."

"I'll be waiting for you," Karen said.

Joanna replaced the receiver and sat thinking. She hadn't seen or heard from Karen in two days and had begun to wonder if Karen had chosen simply to fade out of her life without a word. She had decided not to call Karen, to wait it out and let Karen decide for herself. After all, Joanna reasoned, if Karen wasn't happy with her, she deserved to be wherever she could be happy, and with people who didn't make her feel uncomfortable. The decision had been easier to make than to implement. She missed Karen. No matter how busy her days or evenings, memories of Karen, her touch, her kiss, her laugh, crowded her conscious mind. Everything reminded her of Karen, and without Karen, the whole world seemed flat; food had no taste, music seemed unimportant, nothing seemed funny, and Joanna felt empty.

A glance at her watch told her she had three hours of commitments before she could go home. Home to Karen. Quickly, the thought was replaced with doubts. Who was she kidding? *I'm only getting to borrow her for a couple of days.* As soon as her family returned, she'd be gone again. The thought brought a hollow feeling capable of devouring every ray of hope. She couldn't acquiesce to hopelessness. Seeing Karen now and then was better than not seeing her at all.

Joanna picked up the file on her next patient and began reviewing the history.

Karen used the key Joanna had given her to let herself into Joanna's house. She had stopped at Cloudt's Delicatessen and bought supper — cold lobster, marinated mushrooms, hearts of palm salad, and oil-roasted artichoke hearts. She placed the individual containers in the refrigerator, and laid the already chilled bottle of champagne next to them. She looked at her cache with satisfaction. It had cost quite a bit — almost half of the cash she kept aside for emergencies. Phillip knew nothing of its existence, so it allowed her a little more freedom to follow the dictates of her heart and mind.

Since Joanna would be home in half an hour, Karen had plenty of time to arrange the rest of her surprise. She grabbed the two Rich's department store shopping bags and ran upstairs to Joanna's bedroom. In less than two minutes, she had stripped the bed, tossed the used sheets and pillow cases in the clothes hamper, and relegated the folded spread to the linen closet.

She opened the packages and ran her hands over the pale pink satin sheets and pillow cases. Joanna would love the feel of them against her skin. She made up the bed, then added a featherweight burgundy comforter. Smoothing out the last wrinkles, she stepped back to admire it, her mind filled with images of Joanna and herself making love on the cool smoothness of the sheets and the silken warmth of each other's skin.

She was at the door when she remembered to light a fire in the fireplace. Two medium-sized logs, just enough to add an extra soft warmth to the room.

She stood watching the flames. Now all she needed to make it perfect was Joanna. A shiver of excitement played through her as she remembered the touch of Joanna's lips.

Why can't the world just mind its own business, Karen thought. She could be happy with Joanna if people weren't so nosy. Downstairs, she waited in the living room for Joanna. If she got a divorce, they could see each other on a regular basis until Brad and Eric graduated. Then she could sell the house and move in, if Joanna was willing to wait.

"Karen?" Joanna's voice sounded happy.

"I'm in here," Karen called. They met in the hallway between the living room and the kitchen.

Joanna's smile was a perfect welcome. Karen wrapped her arms around her and yielded willingly to her kiss.

"God, you feel good," Joanna said, rubbing her cheek against Karen's. "I missed you."

"I missed you."

Joanna pulled her closer. She trembled as Joanna slipped her hand under her sweater.

Karen pulled back and looked into Joanna's eyes. "Are you hungry? I brought supper." Karen could feel the heat of Joanna's body against her own. She looked into Joanna's eyes and recognized the love and passion they held for her. "You're not interested in supper right now, are you?"

Joanna shook her head slowly. She leaned forward and kissed her passionately.

"Let's go upstairs," Karen whispered. "I want to feel your skin on mine."

Joanna's bedroom felt warm and golden. The flames from the fireplace, along with the first silver ribbons of moonlight, gave the only light in the darkening room. Shadows undulated across the floor, slid upward along the new burgundy spread, and lay in wide bands across Joanna's bed. Joanna's mouth covered Karen's completely. Her hands traveled from Karen's back to her breasts and shoulders, until tremors of pleasure shot through Karen's body.

"I love you," Joanna whispered. She unbuttoned Karen's sweater and bent to kiss her bare shoulders.

Shadows and light defined Joanna's face, as if the light originated with Joanna, sending its radiance and warmth into the room.

Karen quivered as Joanna unzipped her slacks and pushed them to the floor. Her hands moved up Karen's legs, ever so slowly along her inner thighs. Karen caught her breath as the tips of Joanna's fingers tickled the buttery skin between her legs, spreading the wetness they found along the shaft and tip of Karen's swollen pearl. Karen opened to her like a giant sunflower, enfolding her in a private world known only to her and Joanna.

Joanna's arms felt strong as they swept her up and laid her on the pink satin sheets.

Joanna undressed, then lay down on top of her, enclosing her. Waves of excitement broke inside her as Joanna brushed her lips across her eyelids, her forehead, her cheeks. Karen sighed when Joanna's tongue skimmed across her lips and slipped into her waiting mouth.

"I want you so much," Karen whispered.

She felt Joanna's fingers capture the erect pearl, and then Joanna was kneeling over her, pulling her nipples inside her mouth, one at a time, until they hardened. Joanna moved downward and her fingers pinched her nipples, providing new heights of intensity.

Pleasure filled Karen completely as Joanna continued caressing, stroking and kissing her body. She buried her fingers in Joanna's hair. Like a dancer who had followed her partner's lead many times, Joanna brushed the inside of Karen's thighs with her lips and tongue. Shockwaves of anticipation rippled through Karen, and Joanna brushed her inner lips and clitoris with her passionate tongue.

"Oh, Joanna," Karen moaned. Balanced on the razor's edge of sensation, she moved her hips to meet Joanna's tongue. Suddenly, Joanna enveloped Karen's swollen lips and bulging clitoris, trapping them under her ceaseless tongue.

Karen could feel Joanna's excitement, could hear her sighs. She surrendered completely to Joanna, and pleasure exploded. They were one, hurtling toward the sun. The burning heat seared them into one spiritual entity, more alive together than either was apart.

Joanna lay next to her and kissed her, and Karen could taste her own peachy sweetness on her lips. She pulled Joanna closer. "I love you, Joanna," she whispered. "I love you more than anything else in this world." Karen held Joanna's face in her hands. "I want you."

Joanna moved upward and straddled her. Karen braced her knees against Joanna's back and held her full hips in her hands. She felt her excitement mount as Joanna relaxed and knelt over Karen's mouth. Karen's tongue caressed Joanna's lips, swollen and pink with desire. She circled the erect pearl, stroking it directly with long firm strokes, sucking it inward, and rolling it against her tongue.

Joanna was moaning with pleasure. Her hips pushed fiercely against Karen's mouth, but Karen refused to relent, knowing that she was guiding Joanna past the point of pleasure, into a starburst of ecstasy. Insistently, she took her firmly with her tongue, and Joanna screamed as her body became rigid, shook with pleasure, and she collapsed. Joanna pressed her mouth against Karen's and slid her hands through Karen's hair. Karen felt as if Joanna were kissing places that had never known kisses before.

"I love you, Karen." Joanna's words were barely audible. "I love you."

Karen reached down and pulled the satin sheet and bedspread up to cover them. She pulled Joanna close and kissed her eyes. "I love you, Joanna. I love making love with you."

CHAPTER 17

The sound of the phone pulled Karen out of a deep sleep. She could hear Joanna's voice and rolled over in the direction of the sound. She put her arm around Joanna and pulled herself close. Her body met and followed the curves of Joanna's back and buttocks. She slipped her leg between Joanna's and placed brief, light kisses on Joanna's back.

Suddenly, Joanna moved and lamplight hit Karen in the eyes. The next thing she knew, Joanna had disentangled herself and was sitting up with her back against a pillow and the headboard.

"What I do with my time is none of your business," Joanna snapped.

Karen looked at her watch — 5:10 a.m.

"I don't want to discuss this any further." Joanna sounded angrier by the minute. "No, don't come over here." She sat bolt upright. "You're where? I don't have time, Vicki. Don't come over." Joanna looked at the receiver. "Damn! She hung up."

Joanna was as white as chalk and her eyes had the look of a frightened animal.

"What's wrong?" Karen asked.

"Vicki's on her way over here. She called on her car phone, and should be here in five minutes."

Karen was puzzled by Joanna's apparent fear. "So what's the problem? I can stay up here. Just keep her downstairs. She can't possibly know I'm here. My car's around the corner."

"She claims she's going out of town and needs some of the things she left in her closet."

"At five in the morning? Joanna, why are you so upset? Just let her get her things and get out. I can just stay in here."

"She won't just look in her bedroom." Joanna sounded stressed. "She'll snoop into everything."

"Then don't let her in. Tell her she'll have to tell you what she's looking for and you'll go get it." Karen was surprised at Joanna's reaction. She had never seen her so out of control.

"She has a key. She'll let herself in."

Karen was stunned. "You never changed the locks?"

"I forgot about it. It didn't seem all that important."

Karen got up quickly and pulled her clothes on. "I don't believe this. You let me stay overnight knowing Vicki could walk in any time?"

"The alarm would go off if she opened the door."

"What are you saying? That your overnight guest would have time to hide? That's just great, Joanna."

Suddenly the alarm sounded and was shushed.

"Joanna?" Vicki called from the kitchen.

"Go slow her down while I hide somewhere." Karen urged Joanna toward the door.

"But —"

"Never mind," Karen said. "Just go meet her. I'll take care of myself."

Karen closed the bedroom door and thought about where to hide. Under the bed, in the closet, in the shower? She slid the closet door open and squeezed in behind the jackets, bathrobes, skirts and other clothes. The floor of the closet was littered with shoes, several boxes, and at least two rolled up carpets. She balanced her feet on the two carpets and leaned against the back wall as she slid the closet door closed.

After only one minute, her legs felt cramped and sweat was forming on her forehead. God, she thought, I hope I can stand this heat until she gets her out of here. She started to readjust her position and almost lost her balance, catching herself just before falling off the carpets. Her heart was pounding as she strained to hear. What the hell were they doing?

She didn't have to wait long. She heard the bedroom door opening, followed by Joanna's voice.

"There's nothing of yours in my closet," Joanna said. "I moved everything into your room."

"Well, you don't mind if I look, do you?" Vicki's voice was all too clear.

Suddenly, the closet door slid back, and Karen almost fell. She wavered for a second, then regained her balance. She held her breath as light streamed into the closet and she caught a glimpse of Vicki's arm. A split second later, clothes were moving in her direction. Karen stayed as still as possible, barely allowing herself to inhale. Something moved on the floor and Karen struggled to keep her balance.

If she sees me, Karen thought, I'll yell as loud as I can and make a run for it. She braced herself, ready to spring forward and escape. She blinked several times, trying to clear the sweat from her eyes. Her lungs felt as if they were about to burst. She had to breathe. *If she hears me, I'll deal with it then.* She inhaled as quietly as she could, the deepest breath she had taken in ten minutes. Suddenly she was aware of dust and the smell of mold. Her nose and throat were as dry as sand as she fought her need to cough. Dust tickled her nose and sweat rolled into her eyes again. She raised her right hand slowly and pinched her nose shut, hoping it would kill her need to sneeze or cough.

Suddenly the closet door moved forward and the closet was completely dark again. Dark and hot. Sweat covered Karen's face and trickled down her neck. She could feel her blouse sticking to her back. Dust filled her nose and throat again as she tried to inhale silently. She let her mouth fill with saliva and swallowed hard, hoping to clear the dust and tickle from her throat. Sweat rolled down her chest forming a narrow moving stream between her breasts.

"I have to get dressed." Joanna sounded annoyed. "If you're finished looking, how about leaving so I can get ready for work?"

"What's the hurry?" Vicki's voice strengthened and faded as she spoke.

She must be walking around, Karen thought.

"Joanna, if I ever find out you've been seeing someone behind my back, I'll do everything I can to ruin both of you." Vicki's words started Karen's heart pounding in her ears. "I mean it, Joanna. I won't be made a fool."

"You're the one who decided to move out," Joanna said angrily. "Do you expect me to live the rest of my life alone?"

"No. I know you'll eventually get involved with somebody." Vicki sounded as if she was standing right next to the closet doors. "I just better not find out it was somebody you've been seeing all along. I often wondered about you and that Wainwright woman. I think she was attracted to you."

"God, Vicki!" Joanna sounded indignant. "What I do and who I do it with is none of your business."

"Yes, I know," Vicki said. "It's the only thing that makes me think I'm wrong about you two. I know you'd never live in a house with teenagers, or in a house where you had to be extremely careful about everything you said and did. If it wasn't for that, I'd bet you two were having an affair." Vicki's voice took on a harder edge. "And if I found out that was true, I'd expose the bitch to her husband and her children." Someone snapped her fingers. "That fast, Joanna. I'd make her sorry she ever heard your name."

"Your compassion and understanding have always

impressed me," Joanna said. "Why should that change now?"

"Just remember, I gave you clear warning," Vicki said. "That woman will leave you faster than rats deserting a sinking ship if she thinks her kids will be hurt in any way. Not to mention how she'd feel when she finds she can't get hired anywhere."

"Vicki, I don't have time to listen to this junk," Joanna said. "I have patients waiting."

Karen could hear them moving away from the area in front of the closet. Joanna said, "I'll walk you to your car."

"What about my other sweaters?" Vicki asked, her voice trailing after Joanna.

"If I find them, I'll send them to you. There's no point stopping by again. You've looked through everything."

"Won't you miss me?" Vicki said. Karen heard a door close and the voice stopped.

That bitch, Karen thought. I'd like to wring her neck. She wiped the sweat from her face. The heat in the closet was almost unbearable and her chest hurt. *Come on, Joanna, get back up here so I know it's safe to come out*. Time seemed to drag. *What are you doing, driving her home?*

She heard the bedroom door open.

"Karen?" Joanna called. "Where are you?"

Karen relaxed and felt her knees buckle. She fell sideways against the closet door, caught herself, and pushed the door back.

The bedroom felt luxuriously cool after the cramped closet. Karen stumbled over the rugs she had been standing on and fell headlong onto the bedroom floor.

"Are you okay?" Joanna knelt down and helped Karen. "I'm sorry you were in there so long. Your muscles must really hurt."

Karen put her arms around Joanna's neck and pulled herself to her feet.

"I can't believe that woman gets away with that kind of behavior." Karen was furious at Vicki, at the closet, at Joanna. "I will never do that again for anybody." She looked directly into Joanna's eyes. "I will never hide from that woman again. Not for you, not for anybody."

"I'm sorry, Karen. I can't control her behavior," Joanna said.

"Well, she isn't going to control my behavior either."

"Somehow I already got that impression." Joanna's grin said more than her words.

CHAPTER 18

It had taken two phone calls before Joanna found another doctor to cover for her at the clinic and hospital. Only then, when she was sure she had the time free, did she call Karen.

"That's wonderful," Karen said. "Where should we go?"

"Well, we can fly somewhere or we could just drive to the mountains," Joanna said.

"Let's drive. That way we'll have more time together," Karen said.

They couldn't decide between Sky Valley and Savannah. A toss of the coin sent them happily to Sky Valley.

"I wish it were cold enough for them to make snow," Karen said as she looked toward the main slopes. "Skiing would be fun."

"I guess we'll have to settle for long walks in the woods and a fire at night to take the chill out of the air," Joanna said.

They followed the directions they'd received at the main lodge, and in less than ten minutes were parked beside a three-story chalet overlooking the main slopes.

"This is wonderful," Karen said as she set her suitcase down and began to explore.

A long wall of windows formed one side of the room. "What a lovely view," Karen said. "Come see, Joanna. It's a shame there's no snow."

Joanna admired the green, rolling landscape. Without a person in sight, the scene looked like a painting; a perfect light blue sky melted into the room's two-tone green carpet with Karen in her white pants and rust-colored sweater a part of it.

Joanna felt Karen's hand take hers. "Let's pick out a bedroom."

Joanna followed Karen through the chalet. "This is it," Karen said. "Look at that skylight and that view."

Joanna agreed. This was the best of the four bedrooms. She put her arm around Karen as they looked out the window. She was aware of the crisp, clean scent of Karen's cologne, the memory of Karen's kiss.

She turned to find Karen watching her. Karen's eyes looked bright with passion as she leaned forward and kissed Joanna.

Joanna gathered her in and held her close. She brushed Karen's lips which opened to receive Joanna. With trembling hands, she undressed Karen and teased Karen's erect nipples, then lowered her head and took Karen's nipples, one then the other, into her mouth. Joanna shivered as she slipped her hand over Karen's flat belly to the downy hair and parted wet lips. She moved her fingers slowly along the wet satiny lips. Listening to Karen's sounds of pleasure, she was aware of the rhythmic dance of Karen's hips, aware of the fluttering within her own body.

Joanna guided Karen to a large armchair and knelt in front of her. She pulled Karen's slacks and laced trimmed panties from her body and kissed her way from her stomach to her thighs. At Joanna's touch, Karen's legs opened and allowed Joanna to plant her kisses on Karen's inner thighs.

Karen's fingers gripped the arms of the chair.

Joanna sat back on her heels and looked up at Karen's face. Her hunger showed in her eyes.

Joanna watched as she moved her fingers slowly over Karen's clitoris, its color deepening, her scent rising. Karen caught her breath and her face contorted with pleasure. Joanna knew she had her right on the edge. Karen urged Joanna downward; Karen knew what she wanted.

Joanna's heart was pounding with excitement. She kissed her way to Karen's thighs and upward to the swollen flesh between Karen's thighs. She brushed Karen's lips with her tongue, slowly at first, then faster and more firmly. There was power in this act — an equal exchange of give and take. She knew exactly where Karen was most vulnerable and timed her strokes to match Karen's moans. Finally, Joanna increased her pressure, delivering firmer and faster strokes to Karen's clitoris. Karen bucked in the chair, and she could feel Karen's fingers pushing her head more firmly against her. Joanna moved from side to side, never slowing her pace. She could feel Karen swelling in her mouth, her clitoris firm and sleek. A long, continuous moan signaled the beginning of orgasm, and Karen's body began to shake.

Joanna withheld nothing. She followed Karen's movements perfectly. Then, as if a match had been struck, Joanna's own pleasure burst, joined with Karen's cries of pleasure.

She pulled Karen to the floor and wrapped her arms around her.

"I love you, Karen," Joanna whispered. "I want to share my life with you. I want us to live together."

Karen kissed Joanna, then said softly, "We will. Just give me some time."

They made love several times a day and neither brought up the subject of living together again. It seemed to Joanna that nothing she could say would hasten Karen's leaving Phillip. She resolved to be content with whatever time they could steal.

* * * * *

On Sunday morning, they started back to Atlanta. They had traveled almost ten miles without more than a word or two between them.

Joanna took her eyes off the road to glace at Karen. She was looking straight ahead and seemed deep in thought.

Joanna took Karen's hand. "You seem light-years away. What are you thinking?"

Karen squeezed her hand. "The time went by so fast. I wish it were just beginning instead of ending."

Joanna thought she heard a note of depression in Karen's voice. "We can get together again as often as you want. My schedule is somewhat flexible."

"I'm not sure this is going to work, Joanna. It gets more and more risky each time."

Joanna was stunned. She hoped she had misheard or misinterpreted what Karen had said. She pulled her hand gently from Karen's and tightened her grip on the steering wheel. "I don't think I heard what you said."

"I don't think we should meet again for a while." Karen's voice was cold and hard. "The risks are getting to be too much."

Joanna didn't want to believe what she was hearing and didn't want to feel the pain she knew it would bring. "Which risks are you talking about?"

"The risk of losing my sons if someone tells Phillip or them about us."

Joanna was exerting tremendous control just to keep her voice calm. In her mind's eye, she could see herself moving in faster and faster circles, until suddenly she broke into a thousand pieces and flew off in all directions. She held herself together and calmly asked, "When did you decide this?"

"I've been thinking about it for days." Karen looked at the floor. "I just can't keep taking this kind of risk. Between my nosy neighbors and your crazy ex-lover, Phillip and the boys are bound to find out. If they do, I'll lose my sons. I couldn't take that. They'd be devastated that I had done anything that could lead to them being taken away from me."

Joanna pulled the car into a restaurant parking lot, turned off the engine and turned toward Karen. "When did you decide this?" Joanna repeated her question. She felt devastated and had to know when Karen had actually made up her mind.

"What difference does it make?" Karen said. "My answer won't change anything. I have no grounds to get a divorce from Phillip."

"I need to know, Karen. Did you come up here knowing that you were going to tell me this today?" Joanna wanted to plead with Karen not to make this mistake, but pleading would make things worse.

"I didn't actually decide until we were on our way back." Karen met Joanna's eyes. "I honestly wish there was another way, but there isn't."

"How can you go back to being his wife?" Anger was beginning to choke her.

"I'm going back for Brad and Eric. They need their mother." Karen wiped the tears from her cheeks with her hand.

"Divorce Phillip and bring the boys with you. We can move out of state." Joanna felt as if her heart were breaking.

"The boys will never move away from their

father. Besides, what about your practice? You'd have to start all over again. You have a good practice here. If you moved out of state, it would mean starting all over again. I love you, Joanna. I don't want you to have to go through that."

"Divorce him for irreconcilable differences, for no-fault . . . you and the boys live alone. We can see each other away from your home." Joanna felt she was on the verge of pleading. "It took me so long to find you." Joanna's mind was a kaleidoscope of past and future dreams.

"It wouldn't work, Joanna. Phillip would fight for custody. He'd also do whatever he could to turn the boys against me." Tears were streaming down Karen's face.

"Then there's no hope." Joanna felt hollow. She stretched out her hand and wiped the tears from Karen's eyes. "I love you. I don't want to lose you."

Karen put her hand over Joanna's and pressed it to her cheek. "I love you, too, but I can't leave my children, and I can't take the chance of Phillip finding out about us and taking them away."

CHAPTER 19

In the first two weeks following their breakup, Joanna was consumed with thoughts of Karen. Pictures of the past intruded into her waking hours, pulling her attention and energy backward, while she fought with every weapon at her command to address the events of the present, and to reshape her dreams of the future. The powerful attraction of the past intruded into every conversation, every activity, every situation. There was no day, no hour, without the memory of Karen. Joanna looked for her wherever she went, expecting to see her in a mall, in a store, or in a car next to her at a red light. The possibility of seeing her tore at her like two powerful magnets, each determined to have her in its entirety. Would a glimpse of Karen bring pain or relief? Did she want to run into her, or was she better off without seeing her at all?

"Joanna, you have to stop this craziness," Nancy told her one evening at a restaurant. "Karen has made her choice. You have to respect her wishes." Nancy paused. "And what about Vicki? Have you heard from her again?"

"Every day this week." Joanna didn't want to talk about Vicki any more than she wanted to talk about Karen. She realized however, that Nancy wasn't going to give up.

"What does she want?" Nancy looked skeptical.

"The first time she called, she said she wanted to apologize for barging in last week. The next time, she wanted to know how I was doing." Joanna took a drink of club soda. "The time after that, she wanted to talk about reconciliation."

"Well, isn't that something!" Nancy looked like she was enjoying herself. "What did you tell her?"

"That I didn't think it would work, that we've been through this at least a hundred times, that I hoped we could remain friends." Joanna felt depressed. "It makes me sick to think of all the time we wasted."

"God, even Vicki would be better than Karen," Nancy said. "At least she doesn't have a husband and children to deal with."

Joanna was disgusted. "That's ridiculous. Vicki didn't communicate then and she won't communicate now. She doesn't know how, and she's too threatened by the truth to try to learn." Sadness overwhelmed her. "In so many ways, Vicki's fears and pride are her own worst enemies."

"Then you don't think you two will ever get back together?" Nancy asked, concerned.

"No. It's too late for that. When it comes right down to it, Vicki doesn't really like me much at all."

Joanna looked around the restaurant. She had eaten here with Karen on several occasions and half-expected to find her sitting at a table nearby.

"What are you looking for?" Nancy snapped. "Do you realize you're looking for her even now?" Nancy put her hand on Joanna's arm. "If you continue like this, you won't be able to function as a human being, let alone as a physician." She tapped Joanna's arm. "Hey, remember me? I'm the woman you're supposed to be having dinner with."

Joanna looked at Nancy and forced thoughts of Karen from her mind. "I warned you I wouldn't be good company tonight." She felt pressured and was determined not to give in to it. "I don't feel like having dinner. I don't *feel* like being out." Joanna's anger was returning. Anger at Nancy for pushing her, anger that Karen had chosen Phillip over her, anger that society demanded that Karen conform — and she herself couldn't even fight to keep Karen. "If you're not satisfied with my company, it's your own fault. You're the one who insisted we get together." Joanna wanted to lash out at the world, but Nancy became her target. "You can leave, or even better, I'll leave. I'll call you when I feel better. Maybe you'll have a more enjoyable evening then." She pushed her chair back and started to stand up.

Nancy grabbed her arm. "Please don't leave,

Joanna." She looked panicked. "If I hurt your feelings, I apologize. I didn't mean to." Her eyes pleaded with Joanna. "Please stay."

Humbled by Nancy's obvious care for her, Joanna sat down and took a deep breath. "I'm the one who should apologize. You just caught about six months' worth of anger."

Nancy patted Joanna's arm and flashed a brief smile. "What can I do to help? Just name it and it's done."

Joanna felt warmed by Nancy's willingness to help. She returned her fleeting smile. "I'm not sure anyone can help right now." She felt empty and hopeless. "I really love Karen Wainwright, and losing her is just about killing me." Her throat ached as she fought to contain her tears. Then the battle was over and she could feel their wet heat as they made their way down her face. Her hand trembled as she lifted her glass and took a drink of club soda. "I can't stop thinking about her when I'm awake, and when I go to sleep, I dream about her. I keep telling myself it's only been a week, and things will get better as time passes. But in the meantime, I feel as if I die a little every day."

"Have you tried to talk to her?"

"No. It wouldn't help. If she still chose to stay with Phillip, I'd feel worse. And if I talked her into leaving Phillip and she lost her kids, she'd hate me, and that would be much worse." She leaned back in her chair. "So talking to Karen isn't the solution."

"Does that mean you know what the solution is?"

"No. I wish I did." Joanna shivered as the memory of Karen's kiss filled her mind and moved through her body. "I'm afraid my only hope for peace of mind is to lose myself in my work. It always worked with Vicki. I hope it works with Karen."

"I hope it does too," Nancy said. "I hope something makes you stop hurting." Nancy cleared her throat. "Do you mind if I ask you a personal question?"

"I'll tell you after you ask it," Joanna said, bracing herself.

"I guess I'm curious enough to take my chances. Just what is it that makes Karen Wainwright so important to you, other than the fact that you love her? People fall in and out of love every day, but what you seem to feel for Karen is different."

Joanna sighed. "It's almost as if Karen and I have been lovers before, in the past, and will be again. It wasn't easy to find her this time, and it certainly isn't easy to lose her, especially when I'm positive we were meant to be together."

"What if you're wrong?"

"I'm not wrong. But even if I were, what harm is there in believing?"

"You actually believe that you and Karen have been lovers before?"

"Yes, many times," Joanna said. "And we will be lovers again in the future." She felt a deep sadness. "But maybe not again in this lifetime. I'll have to find her again, and hope again that she recognizes me."

"Recognizes you? How could she recognize you in some other life and time?"

"I believe that souls recognize each other. A shared history strikes a chord. The memory of a kiss convinces you, or the memory of a touch. However it happens, it's as if lovers who've shared their very souls with each other seek and find each other again."

"I hope it works out for you. But you still have a problem in this life. What are you going to do about that?"

She managed a smile. "I'm going to dive into my work and pray that the sound of my own splashing will drive the memory of Karen out. At least until I'm able to deal with it again."

CHAPTER 20

In the first two months after her breakup with Joanna, Karen learned what being a martyr really meant. It was nothing like the stories of martyrs that the nuns had read to her and her classmates as children. In those versions, no matter how bad the suffering, the martyrs always found something to be happy about. They joked while being roasted alive, they sang hymns while lions pulled them apart, they smiled while being beheaded. Karen learned quickly that 20th-century martyrdom has no resemblance to childhood stories.

Returning to roles she had never liked was more difficult now that she knew what life could be like without them. She had had a glimpse of what a relationship could offer when it was really right, and like it or not, that glimpse had become the standard against which she measured all other relationships. She frequently recalled a line she had read years ago: "Eyes once opened can never close completely again." Knowing there was something better made it nearly impossible to accept what she was determined to settle for.

She felt as if she were divided against herself. Like pieces of a mosaic, desire, hatred, resignation, and memories battled for the right to form the pattern of her life, patterns which shifted easily and daily. "Settling" could never be easy or painless.

Karen tried to become more of everything her societal roles demanded. She insisted that she prepare breakfast every morning, pack a lunch for the boys, and cook supper every night.

"I'm not eating this," Brad complained. "You burned the eggs again." He threw his fork down on his plate. "Why don't you just let Dad take us to McDonald's?"

"Brad, don't talk to your mother like that." Phillip's voice was calm, almost gentle. "If she wants to cook for us, this is where we eat."

"I don't see why we have to change our lives because she decided all of a sudden she wants to play mother." He looked at Karen. "You're ruining things." Brad's voice was angry. "We like going to breakfast with Dad. It has nothing to do with you. Why don't you just leave us alone? Go back to the

Women's Clinic. We don't need you. You just mess things up."

Karen felt like an observer watching some awful soap opera. She had worked so hard at putting her feelings to sleep that she felt no pain at Brad's words, only the awareness that she should be hurt. It was like looking down and discovering that your foot was bleeding without ever feeling the nail or glass that had ripped it open.

She wanted to say something to Brad, something to make his adolescent rebellion go away. The mosaic shifted again, and she remembered the first time she saw hatred in her son's eyes. He had loved her before, hadn't he? Loved her as any child loves his mother. What had changed?

"Now, Brad, you can't talk to your mother like that." Phillip's voice was another from the soap opera. "Mind your manners."

"Mom, are you all right?" Eric's voice cut through the fog that pinned Karen outside time. Time that moved by her like a river, rushing by the rocks and boulders in its path, washing them, pushing them, surrounding them, but leaving them where they stood, essentially unchanged.

"I'm fine." Karen could hear the flatness in her own voice. None of them are sensitive enough to hear it, she thought.

"You ought to slap him when he talks to you like that." Eric glared at Brad.

"We don't hit in this family." Phillip's voice entered from somewhere outside the fray. He was always announcing new rules or principles when the ones he had announced previously no longer worked

167

for him. He was stroking his beard and looking smug. What's missing from this picture, Karen asked herself. The cream mustache of a satisfied cat, or a yellow canary feather or two clinging to his beard?

"You boys get your things and wait for me in the car. I'll be right there." Phillip's voice was syrupy.

A smile slipped across Brad's face as he slid from his chair. "Sure, Dad. But don't take too long. We still have time to stop by McDonald's if we hurry."

"See you later, Mom," Eric said.

Phillip didn't say a word while the boys were gathering up their books and jackets. Karen followed the sounds and knew where each was, and how close they were to being ready. They walked through the kitchen stopping only to kiss Karen on the cheek, a ritual taught to them when they were still toddlers. "Always kiss your mother before you leave the house in the morning," Phillip would say as soon as they could understand. "It shows your respect for her."

The sound of the door closing seemed to be a signal for Phillip, as if someone had shouted, "Lights, camera, action."

He stopped stroking his beard and leaned toward her. His expression looked remarkably like the one she had seen on Brad's face minutes ago.

"I'm tired of your excuses. You don't feel well, you're too tired, you're just not in the mood." Phillip's voice was sharp and hard. "I'll be in San Antonio for five days. When I get back, I expect you to start acting like my wife. Talk to your shrink or whoever, but make up your mind that ours is not going to be a sexless marriage. You made certain commitments when you married me, and if you're

168

not going to keep them, I think we need to have a serious talk." His eyes narrowed to puffy slits. "Do you hear me Karen? I want you to understand that I'm not kidding."

Karen felt a large knot form in her stomach. The pain had started as soon as she'd heard the words "serious talk." A serious talk with Phillip always meant him telling her where she failed as a wife and mother, and how lucky she was to have a family who cared enough about her to make allowances. From there, he'd move into his "men and women are different" dissertation, pointing out that it could actually cause physical damage to a man if he went without sex too long or too often. There was no point in telling him that scientific evidence did not support his argument, since, according to Phillip, "his own experience was worth a hundred scientific experiments."

Karen felt trapped. The thought of Phillip touching her made her physically sick, but so did the thought of neighbors pointing her out as some kind of unnatural creature who had chosen a woman for her lover and partner, and forsaken her husband and children. No one would forgive her for that — least of all, herself. She wanted, even longed for, a life with Joanna, but common sense told her that the road would lead to ostracism. If only she could feel more for Phillip. She wanted to fit the roles society had assigned her, if only she could find some joy in them. It wasn't natural for a wife not to desire her husband. Why couldn't things be different? Why couldn't she just forget Joanna and be happy with Phillip?

"Do you understand me, Karen?" Phillip asked the question as if he were speaking to someone from another country. "The boys and I need more attention from you."

"Yes, Phillip, I understand completely." Karen felt totally defeated. There was no real choice. She wasn't about to leave her children for anyone or anything. Not even her own happiness. She'd try harder with Phillip. After all, he wasn't a monster. He didn't beat her, he came home every night, and he didn't play around on the side. She owed him a sex life, whether her heart was in it or not.

Phillip had put his jacket on. "I'll call you in a day or so, just to make sure everything is going all right." He looked directly at Karen. "I meant what I said, Karen. When I get back, I expect you to act like my wife." He took her hand. "Now, walk me to the door and tell me you'll miss me."

The words stuck in Karen's throat like sun-baked clay. The pain was worse, and she felt sure she was going to throw up. Large, hot tears rolled from the corners of her eyes.

Phillip put his arms around her and pulled her close. "It's all right. You don't have to say anything. I can see that you'll miss me." He pushed his mouth against hers and shoved his tongue inside. His beard pricked her skin and the force of his kiss actually hurt.

He let her go and smiled at her. "We could have this kind of passion all the time, if you'd just cooperate a little." He shoved his mouth at her again. His lips felt hard and hot as he pushed his tongue into her mouth again. "There," he said as he released her and stepped back. "Think about that while I'm gone and we won't need that serious talk."

The door closed behind him and Karen ran to the bathroom and threw up.

CHAPTER 21

Karen looked at her watch and thought about calling Phillip. He had been in San Antonio for two days and she was trying to remember his schedule. If she called him after 7:30 a.m., they'd have to call him out of a seminar.

"Why is it taking so long?" Eric asked for the third time in ten minutes. He sounded tired and tense. "They've been operating on Brad for an hour. How long does it take to take an appendix out?"

Karen looked at her son. He had stopped pacing

and was standing in the doorway of the surgical waiting room.

"They should be finished soon," Karen said. "Come sit down over here."

Eric slumped next to Karen on the beige vinyl-covered sofa. "Is Brad going to be okay, Mom?"

Karen put her arm around Eric's shoulders and hugged him. "Brad will be fine." No sooner were the words out of her mouth than the thought of peritonitis crossed her mind. Let it be a simple appendectomy, she thought.

"I wish Dad was here. Brad really wanted him when they told him he had to be operated on." Eric rested his head against Karen's shoulder.

"I'm sure Dad will get back as soon as he can." Karen kissed Eric on the top of the head. "I'll call him as soon as Brad is out of surgery."

"Mrs. Wainwright, I'm Beverly Kelly."

Karen looked up and saw a tall, thin nurse seating herself across from them. She was dressed in OR greens and her hair and shoes were still covered with green surgical garments.

"Everything went fine. Brad's in the recovery room. It will probably be a couple of hours before he's out from under the anesthesia."

Karen felt her body relax. "Thank you," she said to the nurse.

"Why don't you two get some breakfast and come back around eleven o'clock. He should be in his own room by then and you'll be able to see him."

"Fine. That will give me enough time to call my husband." She looked at Eric. "And to get you something to eat."

"Brad's going to be all right?" Eric asked.

Karen hugged him. "Brad is going to be fine. In a few weeks, he'll be as good as new."

The Waffle House was about half full. Karen and Eric took a booth by the window and ordered.

"I'd better call your father and let him know what's happening," Karen said. "I won't be long."

At the pay phone in the back of the restaurant, she gave the operator the credit card number and waited. The hotel room was answered on the third ring. A woman's voice said, "Mr. Wainwright's room."

Karen was surprised to hear a woman. "Mr. Wainwright, please," she said calmly.

"This is the maid. Mr. Wainwright went to get coffee. He'll be right back. Do you want to talk to Mrs. Wainwright?"

Karen was stunned. Could Phillip be so foolish as to share a hotel room with a woman?

"Yes," Karen said. "Tell her Northside Hospital in Atlanta is on the phone."

There was a loud clunk as the maid laid the receiver down. Karen could hear her calling to someone. "Mrs. Wainwright. Northside Hospital in Atlanta says they need to talk to you or Mr. Wainwright."

For a minute, there was the din of muffled voices, then another loud clunk. "She can't come to the phone right now. She said to take a number and Mr. Wainwright will call you when he gets back."

Karen made a quick decision and gave the

number of the pay phone to the maid. "Thank you," Karen added.

She stood in front of the phone, not daring to return to Eric until she was in better control of herself. Her heart was pounding in her ears. That bastard, she thought. All those trips out of town. All the extended weekends. Karen wanted to hit something. Was "Mrs. Wainwright" someone he picked up for a night, or someone he traveled with regularly? She wanted to see Phillip face to face, to watch his expression as he answered her questions. Should she confront him on the phone or wait until he returned to Atlanta? Could she speak with him by phone and act as if nothing were wrong? She clenched her fist and took a deep breath. I'll manage, she told herself. She wanted to confront him in person.

She had just decided to return to Eric when the phone rang, startling her, and her heart began to pound wildly as she lifted the receiver.

"Hello," Karen said calmly.

"Karen, is that you?" Phillip sounded surprised. "The maid said Northside Hospital called. Are you all right?"

"She misunderstood. I told her I'd be returning to the hospital in half an hour." Karen kept her tone matter-of-fact. "Brad had an appendectomy this morning. He'll be fine, but I wanted to let you know. He's been asking for you."

"I can get a plane this afternoon if you think I should come home," Phillip said.

"When were you planning to come back?" Karen asked.

"The day after tomorrow. I can be in Atlanta around two."

"You may as well finish your conference." Karen fought her desire to confront him here and now. "Brad will be fine. I'll tell him you'll see him in a couple of days."

"Well, if you're sure he's all right." Phillip sounded relieved. "It would give me a chance to finish my work here."

"That will be fine, Phillip." Karen exerted all the discipline she could muster.

"Now, you won't be able to reach me after this morning. We're going to finish up the seminar at some bank president's ranch outside of San Antonio. We'll be there until I leave for the plane. Does that make any difference to my staying?" Phillip's voice sounded a little shaky.

Karen swallowed her anger. "None at all," she said. "I can handle things here."

"Good girl. I'll see you in a couple of days." He hung up.

Karen slammed down the receiver and stood there trembling with anger. How dare he treat her like some idiot? If he was playing around, he was going to get more than he bargained for.

Karen had decided to wait until Brad was out of the hospital before confronting Phillip about his San Antonio escapade. She had gotten through the "glad to see you" hug and kiss when Phillip arrived, suitcase in hand, in Brad's hospital room Sunday evening, and she felt pretty sure she could brazen it

176

through the few days and nights before Brad's release. What she wasn't ready for was Phillip's insistence that he spend the night with Brad "to catch up on time lost while I was out of town." Karen had started to tell him how ridiculous that would be when it occurred to her that if Phillip was sleeping at the hospital with Brad, he wouldn't be sleeping with her. With that realization, she kept her mouth shut and told Brad she'd see him in the morning.

"Do you mind taking my suitcase home?" Phillip asked. "In fact, let me change my clothes and you can drop my suit off at the cleaners in the morning."

"No problem," Karen said. "I just want to be home in time to fix Eric his dinner."

Phillip took a pair of slacks and a sports shirt from his suitcase, changed his clothes and handed his suitcase and the suit he had been wearing to Karen.

There was another round of ritual kisses and Karen was out of Brad's room and on her way home. She dropped Phillip's suit while she was exiting the elevator, scooped it up quickly and headed for the door to the parking lot.

"Excuse me." A man's voice came from behind her. She turned to see the security guard walking quickly toward her.

"You dropped something." He handed her Phillip's gray vest from his three-piece suit, and two airline tickets.

"Thanks," Karen said, pushing the vest under her arm. She looked at the tickets in her hand.

"Wouldn't want to lose those." The security guard grinned.

"No, certainly not," Karen said. "Thanks again."

She made it to her car without dropping anything else, threw the suitcase and suit in the back seat, and then realized she still had Phillip's ticket in her hand. Don't tell me he's already booked for his next trip, Karen thought. With a mixture of anger and annoyance, she opened the tickets and read the dates. She looked again. The dates were identical. "What the hell . . ." *Mr. Phillip Wainwright and Ms. Gail Donaldson.* She felt as if a bomb had exploded inside her. Her heart was beating against her chest like a frightened bird trying to find its way out of a cage. Pictures of Gail Donaldson appeared in her mind as if someone were showing her old home movies: Gail Donaldson lighting the candles on their boys' fifth birthday cake; Gail Donaldson and Phillip seated at the piano together at Christmas; Gail and Bob Donaldson's fourteenth wedding anniversary; Gail Donaldson and Karen putting up decorations for the tennis club dance.

Gail Donaldson and Phillip Wainwright making love in San Antonio.

Karen pulled several tissues from a box on the seat next to her and wiped the tears from her eyes and face. She looked at the tickets again. The type was blurred through her tears, but she could still make out the name Gail. She crumpled the tickets and threw them against the windshield. They bounced off and fell to the floor on the passenger's seat.

How could I be so stupid? She had never even suspected that Phillip was seeing anyone, let alone someone the boys used to call Aunt Gail.

178

The thought sent sparks up her spine. She felt like running in all directions at once, screaming until there was no more anger and hurt left inside her. I really want to hit him, Karen thought. I want to smash his face. She clenched her fists and pounded the steering wheel. How could he do this? She hit the steering wheel again and again, screaming at the top of her lungs, "I'd like to kill you for this, Phillip!"

Finally, her hands and throat were too sore to continue. She rested her head against the back of her seat. *Where do I go from here?* She caught sight of the crumpled airline tickets and suddenly she knew what she had to do.

Karen parked the car in the driveway and went immediately to the kitchen telephone.

Nervously, she listened to the ring. It was taking all the discipline she could gather not to be hitting something or telling Phillip what she thought of him. A woman's voice answered on the third ring.

"Hello," Karen said in as friendly a voice as she could manage. "Gail? This is Karen Wainwright."

"Hi, Karen," Gail said. "How are you? It's been a long time."

"Too long," Karen said. "That's why I'm calling. How about coming over for coffee in the morning? I thought I'd invite a few of our old tennis club crowd. Can you make it around nine?"

"I don't see why not," Gail said. "It sounds like fun. Maybe we can get back to a regular weekly tennis game."

Karen wanted to scream at Gail. She wanted to say what she thought of her for playing around with Phillip. She pushed the anger down and spoke as if nothing were wrong. "That would be great. I haven't played in so long, I may have forgotten how."

Gail laughed. "It's just like swimming or sex, it will come right back to you."

Karen clenched her fist. God, she wanted to hit this woman. "I hope you're right," Karen said. "At any rate, I'll be looking forward to seeing you in the morning."

"Me, too. It'll be fun to catch up on the latest gossip," Gail said.

Karen's next call was to Brad's hospital room. Phillip answered the phone.

"We're playing gin," Phillip said. "Your son is beating the socks off me."

"Well, I'd like to borrow my son's father in the morning for a leisurely breakfast," Karen said. "Do you think that might be possible? Around eight-thirty?"

"So you did miss me." Phillip sounded self-satisfied.

"Of course I missed you." Karen said sweetly. "Do we have a date?"

"Sure. But I don't have any wheels over here. Are you going to pick me up?" Phillip sounded excited.

"Be at the parking lot at eight-fifteen," Karen said.

"I'll be there. And Karen, I'm glad you took our little talk seriously."

"Me too," Karen said. "See you in the morning." She hung up, hoping the nausea would pass quickly.

God, I'd like to kill him, she thought. He has the nerve to lecture me after what he's been doing.

I know I haven't been an angel, she told herself, but I wasn't lecturing him and criticizing him every time he turned around. She got up and fixed herself a cup of instant coffee. Was she the pot calling the kettle black? Somehow that didn't assuage her anger. She tried to figure out why she felt that what Phillip did was so much worse than what she'd been doing with Joanna. It's his damn hypocrisy, she reminded herself. Phillip only cared about appearances. A knot had formed in the pit of her stomach. She wasn't much better, but at least she cared about the effects on her children.

Karen heard the door open and turned to see Eric walk into the kitchen.

"Hi, Mom." He kissed her on the cheek. "How's Brad?" He opened the refrigerator, poured himself a glass of orange juice, and sat down next to Karen.

"He's doing fine. Daddy is over there. He's spending the night with him."

"Really?" Eric looked impressed. "That's neat. When is Dad coming home?"

"Tomorrow morning." Karen watched her son. "Are you hungry?"

"I ate at Don's house. Could I go over and see Dad and Brad? I don't have to stay long. I'd just like to see him."

"Don't you have homework to do?" Karen felt disappointed that Eric was so anxious to see Phillip.

"Yeah, but I could do it later." Eric didn't sound very determined.

"You can see your father tomorrow when you get home from school."

181

"Okay." He drained his glass. "I guess I'll do my homework."

Karen put her hand on Eric's arm. "Wait a minute. I want to ask you something."

Eric looked at his mother. "What?"

"Daddy and I have had some problems lately." Karen felt uncomfortable with the subject. She wished she could leave the kids out of it.

"Yeah, so?" Eric said.

"It's possible we'll have to separate. Your Dad will probably be moving somewhere else."

"Why?" Eric sounded angry. "Why does Dad have to leave?"

"Sometimes people can't live together," Karen said carefully. "You and your brother and I will stay here in the house. You won't have to give up your friends or your school."

"What if Daddy wants the house? What if Brad and I want to stay here with Daddy?"

Karen felt stunned. She had not even guessed this possibility. "Is that what you want, Eric? To live here with your father and brother?"

Eric blushed. "I don't want to hurt your feelings, but Dad does things with us." He fidgeted in his chair for a moment. "I know Brad wants to stay with Dad. We've talked about it before. Dad's mentioned it too. He said he'd stay here with us."

Karen felt devastated. She had left Joanna to be with her children. How could it be that they didn't want to be with her? How did this get to be a possibility?

"When did Dad talk to you about this?"

"I don't know. A year ago? And then when you got involved with Dr. Jordan's clinic. You were gone

182

most of the time. I think we pretty much felt you were letting everything else go to do the clinic stuff. Will you get divorced? Why can't you live here even if you get a divorce? I don't see why you have to change everything. We like it the way it is. It doesn't seem fair that just because you're not happy, everything has to change."

Karen felt so hurt she was almost numb. "Are you sure you wouldn't want to live with me, Eric?"

"I love you, Mom. I want to be able to see you, but I'd rather live with Dad. We have more things in common." He was quick to add, "But we both want to visit you a lot. We wouldn't have to do that if you'd just change your mind."

Karen shook her head. She didn't know what else to say.

"I'd better go do my homework." Eric stood up. Stuffing his hands in the pockets of his jeans, he said anxiously, "I hope you're not mad at me."

Karen got up and hugged him. "I'm not mad at you. I just want you and your brother to be happy."

"Good," Eric said. "Brad and I will visit you a lot." He kissed Karen and left the kitchen.

Karen sat unmoving, wounded and confused by Eric's words. How could she have missed this attitude in her sons? How could she fail to recognize that they had left her long before she decided to take the steps to leave their father? Answers came slowly, like the first drops of blood from a new wound. She closed her eyes and bit back the excruciating pain that filled her.

Feeling has its price, she thought. When she numbed her feelings for Phillip, she numbed her feelings for everything. She hadn't even seen her own sons slipping away from her. Doctor Wade was right. No one could turn off one or two essential feelings without turning them all off. Running away from pain, blocking her feelings so Phillip couldn't hurt her, put her out of touch with her own sons. The realization was like a razor-sharp sword plunging again and again into her heart. Oh God, she thought, living with Phillip has cost me my sons. Settling for what I thought I had has left me with nothing.

CHAPTER 22

Phillip closed the door behind them. "I think I'll take a quick shower."

"That's fine," Karen said. "Breakfast should be ready about nine."

"Good." Phillip kissed Karen on the cheek.

Karen listened to Phillip's footsteps as he climbed the stairs. She looked at her watch. 8:50 a.m. Gail should arrive any minute. She checked the coffee maker, set the cream and sugar on the table, and sat down to wait.

She had spoken with Eric again over an early breakfast. He had reiterated what he had said the previous evening, adding only that he and Brad had spoken several times about the fact that their parents didn't get along very well, and probably would get a divorce someday. They had worried about what would happen to their father, since he seemed to depend on her so much. "I'm glad Daddy will keep the house," Eric had said, "because everything's close by."

Karen took a sip of her coffee. She still felt devastated at the thought of her sons choosing to live with their father. The knowledge took a lot of the wind out of her confrontation. She could hardly ask Phillip *and* the boys to leave.

There was a knock on the door and Gail Donaldson walked into the kitchen.

"Yoo-hoo. Karen," Gail called.

"Come in, Gail. I've been waiting for you," Karen said. She studied Gail for a moment. She was an attractive woman, about five feet-seven, a hundred and twenty pounds. Her dark wavy hair was short and neat, and her pale blue eyes were large with long lashes.

Gail went to the coffee machine, poured herself coffee and sat down next to Karen. "It's good to see you." Gail leaned over and pecked Karen on the cheek. "Betty Myers told me last night that Brad's in the hospital. Why didn't you say something?" She took a swallow of coffee and reached for the sugar bowl. "You still make the strongest coffee in Georgia." She looked at Karen. "I had a bunch of balloons sent to Brad. They should deliver them this morning."

Karen felt like a cat with a mouse. In the back of her mind, she saw Gail's face go chalk-white when she told her she knew about her and Phillip.

"Any hot gossip to share?"

"You know I really never have dealt in gossip."

Karen heard Phillip coming down the stairs. Her heart was beating faster. It would only be a minute or so now.

"Karen," Phillip called from the hallway. "I'm starving. I hope breakfast is ready."

Karen watched Gail as Phillip entered the kitchen. There was a split second of surprise and her face returned to normal.

"Phillip," Gail said. "Karen didn't tell me you were here. How have you been?"

"Fine. How are you and Bob doing?" Phillip looked at the empty stove top. "I thought you were fixing breakfast, Karen." He poured himself coffee and sat down opposite Gail. "Where's breakfast?"

Karen looked at Phillip in silence. She could see the tiny beads of sweat that were forming on his brow and at the corners of his mustache.

"Can I help, Karen? I'd be happy to scramble some eggs for everyone." Gail's voice sounded shaky.

Karen reached into the pocket of the jacket she was wearing and threw two photocopies on the table.

"How did you like San Antonio, Gail?" Karen divided her attention between Gail and Phillip. Gail's face had turned a pasty gray.

"San Antonio?" she asked. "I've never been to San Antonio."

Phillip picked up the copies, read them and threw them onto the table again. "Where did you get the tickets?" Phillip was on the offense.

"You gave them to me, darling." Karen watched the sweat roll down Phillip's temples.

"I couldn't have given . . ." A look of recognition filled Phillip's eyes. "My suit," he said. "They were in the pocket of my suit."

"Bingo!" Karen said. "I'd like to know how long this has been going on."

Gail picked up the copies and read them. "Oh, my God." Gail's face was indeed like chalk. "Bob mustn't find out about this. Do you hear me, Phillip? You promised me no one would find out."

Phillip's face was scarlet. "Shut up, Gail. Bob isn't going to find out." He turned toward Karen. "What are you after here?"

"The truth," Karen said. "How long have you been involved?"

Phillip looked down. "About two years."

Karen fought to conceal her shock. "Two years," she repeated. "All the time you were nagging me about wanting a better sex life. All the time you were telling me I wasn't giving you and the boys enough attention. All the time you were complaining about all the late hours and all the trips out of town."

"Believe me, Karen, this was never anything serious." Gail's voice was high-pitched and shaky. "Neither of us wants a divorce."

"Really? Why not?" Karen's words were as pointed as she could make them. "Wasn't it what you expected?"

"Don't act like a whore," Phillip growled. "Have some pride here."

Karen's anger burst into rage. She leaned toward Phillip. "Don't you dare talk to me like that. If there's a whore at this table, it isn't me. You know, Phillip, men as well as women can be whores."

She turned to Gail. "You may not want a divorce, but I do." She pushed her chair back and stood up.

"You'd better rethink that," Phillip said with the nervousness of a convict awaiting execution. "You won't get the boys. I've seen to that. They'll choose me, not you."

"I'll be back for my things later." She walked toward the door.

"You can't just walk out. You're my wife." Phillip looked pitiful and scared. "You'll regret this."

"I regret that I stayed this long." Karen opened the door.

"Karen, please don't get Bob involved in this." Gail's mascara was crisscrossed down her cheeks by the wet track of tears. "Please don't."

"I don't intend to talk to Bob." Karen looked at Phillip. "Unless Phillip insults me to my children." She pulled the door shut behind her.

The morning air felt good on her face.

CHAPTER 23

By early afternoon, Karen finally decided that she wouldn't return to the house for another day or two. She had packed a small bag and put it in the trunk of her car before confronting Phillip and Gail, so there was no need to return immediately, even for clothes. She registered at the Marriott Hotel at Lenox Square, freshened up in her room, and went to Northside Hospital to see Brad.

"Hi, Mom." Brad seemed happy to see her. "I thought you'd be here before now."

She kissed him on the cheek. "I had a few things to do this morning."

"Did you remember my magazines," Brad asked.

"Of course." Karen opened her purse and handed him a copy of *Popular Mechanics* and *Sports Illustrated.*

"Thanks," Brad said. "Would you bring me some frozen yogurt when you come back tonight?"

"Why don't you call Dad and ask him to bring it. I probably won't be back until tomorrow morning." She handed Brad a piece of paper. "I need a little time to myself, so I'm staying at the Marriott for a couple of days. This is the phone number in case you need me."

"Why are you doing that? Did you and Dad have a fight?" Brad looked concerned.

"Sort of, but it's nothing for you to worry about. I just need some time to myself." Karen tried to keep her tone casual. Her thoughts were not easy to control. This is terrible, she thought. She was telling half truths and plain lies. But she could explain more later, when he was out of the hospital, when she had had time to plan her strategy.

"Oh." Brad seemed satisfied with her answer. "Well, bring me *Road and Track* when you come tomorrow."

"Okay," Karen said, but in her mind, she fought against concealing the truth. She couldn't tell a sixteen-year-old that she felt as if some monstrous pair of hands had torn her life into pieces and tossed them into the air. What could she say? Don't worry, Brad, your mother is just having a major life crisis at the moment and doesn't feel as if anything in her life is solid? If the situation was difficult for her to deal with, it would be impossible for Brad. Actually, she was surprised that Eric had managed as well as he had, but he always seemed more mature than Brad, more sensitive to her emotional landscape.

"Mom, do you mind if I turn on the television? There's a soccer game on." Brad's fingers were already on the remote control.

She kissed him on the cheek. "You go ahead and watch your game, and I'll see you tomorrow morning."

"Great, Mom, see you then." Brad clicked on the set and was instantly engrossed in the game.

An hour later, Karen turned on the TV in her hotel room and sipped the white wine room service had delivered along with a turkey sandwich. She ran through the channels until she heard the voice of Monica Kauffman, anchorwoman for WSB-TV. She was in the middle of a story about a local car dealer who had been shot and wounded by an unhappy customer.

Karen bit into her sandwich and wondered why anyone would shoot somebody over a substandard tune-up. Her thoughts drifted to Phillip. Maybe he'd give up the boys in exchange for the house. Knowing Phillip, he had a price for everything. It was a matter of finding it. Frustrated, Karen wished there were ready-made answers.

She looked at the handful of mail she had dropped on the bed. The second envelope from the top was clearly addressed in Joanna's handwriting, but with no name or return address. Karen opened it slowly and withdrew a single sheet of wispy lavender note paper. The message read:

What has been will always be,
What you have given now belongs to me.
Not even you can take away
My memories of yesterday.

There was no signature. Karen read and reread the lines. *My memories of yesterday.* A heavy sadness descended on her. Had they lost everything forever? Karen's thoughts were like swords thrust into her consciousness. How could life be so complicated? They loved each other. If only she weren't so concerned with what other people thought. What good did it do her anyway? She'd be divorced and people would think what they wanted.

Suddenly, Monica Kauffman was saying something about an anti-abortion demonstration at the Women's Clinic. She put the note down and paid attention to the TV screen.

"The demonstration got out of hand when picketers attempted to block the entrance of the clinic and prevented women from entering or leaving the clinic building."

A newsreel showed a group of demonstrators swarm around three women walking toward the building. There was a great deal of pushing and shoving as Monica Kauffman continued to narrate: "Atlanta Police moved in quickly and made several arrests."

The crowd shifted and Karen sat up straight and

moved closer to the screen. *Joanna.* The recognition hit her like a thunderbolt.

"Among those arrested was Doctor Joanna Jordan, Director of the Downtown Women's Clinic, and a staunch pro-choice advocate."

Spellbound, Karen watched as two policemen handcuffed Joanna and escorted her to a waiting police van.

A Channel Two reporter thrust a microphone in front of Joanna's face. "Doctor Jordan, what does it feel like to be arrested so many times?"

Joanna looked into the camera. "Being arrested isn't pleasant, but there's little choice when people want to force their beliefs on others by using illegal means and physical violence."

"So you're pretty much resigned to spending the next couple of hours in jail?"

"Unfortunately, our attorney and most of our staff are away at a conference, so I'll probably be spending the night."

The two policemen bustled her into the van.

"There you have it, ladies and gentlemen. Doctor Joanna Jordan will most likely spend tonight in the Atlanta City Jail. The applause and cheers you hear are from anti-abortion demonstrators who, if they had their way, would keep Doctor Jordan in jail for good."

Karen was furious. "Don't count on it," she said to the TV screen. She got up and grabbed her jacket.

* * * * *

"Yes, ma'am, can I help you?" A large black man wearing sergeant's stripes looked over his desk and down at Karen.

Karen didn't know exactly how one was supposed to go about such things, but she was determined to succeed. "Yes, Sergeant, you can. I'm here to pay Doctor Jordan's bail and have her released."

"Just a minute." The Sergeant looked through several papers and handed them to Karen. "Fill these out and return them to me. It's two hundred dollars."

Karen felt doubly gratified that she had withdrawn half of their joint checking account and half their savings account, and had opened her own accounts at another bank. If she had waited, Karen thought, Phillip would have closed the accounts and used the money to control her.

She filled out the forms, made out a check, and handed everything to the Sergeant.

He glanced at the paperwork. "It will take about thirty minutes to get her cleared." He pointed to a door at the far right. "When she's released, she'll come out that door."

"Thank you," Karen said, and sat on the bench at the side of the door the Sergeant had indicated.

She glanced at her watch. Almost 7:00 p.m. At least Joanna hadn't had to stay in jail as long as the time they were both arrested, Karen thought. She relaxed against the back of the bench and allowed her mind to fill with memories. It was like watching a movie as scenes rolled through her and rekindled old feelings. Suddenly Karen was back to the first time she met Joanna. She could see the demonstrators clearly as they pushed and shoved in front of the Women's Clinic. She could see Joanna sitting next to her in the police van that brought them both to jail. God, that seems so long ago, Karen thought.

Newer memories took control and Karen could see Joanna seated at her desk, sunlight streaming through the window behind her. Karen felt her stomach muscles tighten as she remembered watching Joanna and wanting so badly to touch her. She took a deep breath as memories of Pittsburgh played across her mind. She shivered, remembering the soft warmth of Joanna's mouth against her own. She could almost feel Joanna's hands move against her skin.

She imagined her own hands on Joanna's inner thighs. The warm fragrance of musk, and the sweet, salt taste of Joanna played across her senses. A picture of Joanna's smile, and the sound of Joanna's voice filled her mind.

The touch of something sharp against her hand returned her to the present. She pulled the offending object from her jacket pocket and recognized the light lavender color of Joanna's note. She unfolded the paper and reread its message.

How could I forget, she thought. How could she not remember what they'd shared? She felt closer to this woman than she'd ever felt to anyone else in her life. For a moment, Karen knew only sensations of love, warmth, arousal, loneliness, loss — all came tumbling into her heart and mind. The idea of life without Joanna was almost unbearable, the emptiness and loneliness too profound to comprehend. To let Joanna go would mean accepting

196

mere existence instead of really living — for whatever time she had left, one month, one year, twenty years, forty years. The enormity of that realization sparked a light in the darkness of confusion that had confounded Karen for weeks.

She'd already lost her husband, her home, and her children. She'd have to be absolutely crazy to give up Joanna too. My God, she thought, I love the woman so much that I literally risked everything for her — my family, my friends, my way of life. Nobody did that for someone who didn't matter, or for someone who represented just a casual affair. Karen sat up straight. Why should she give her up now? The rough parts were over. She felt warm and light. She wanted to love her, to live with her. She would take her chances and tell her how she felt. If Joanna had changed her mind, or was angry, Karen would ask for another chance.

There was the sound of a sliding bolt. Karen turned in time to see the door open.

Karen stood up. "Joanna," she called in a quiet voice.

Joanna turned toward her immediately. "Karen!" Her voice was filled with joy and surprise. She took several steps and wrapped her arms around Karen. "God, you feel good." She took a step back. "Did you bail me out?" She asked incredulously. "Where's your family? How did you get the money?"

Karen felt in control for the first time in months. "We can talk about all that later," she said. "I have something to tell you and something to ask you."

Joanna sobered. "Go ahead, I'm listening."

Karen spoke softly, keeping her words between herself and Joanna. "I love you, Joanna. I want to build a life with you." She felt pulled to Joanna's eyes as if some great cosmic force guided them both. "Will you forgive me for the way I acted? I want to start a life with you beginning right now. I know there will be problems, a divorce could be pretty messy, and the boys have already decided they want to be with their father. I'm willing to tackle the problems as they come. Are you still interested in a life with me?"

Joanna stood motionless for a second, her light green eyes filled with tears as she put her arm around Karen's shoulders. "You won't have to face the problems alone." She hugged Karen closer. "Let's go home. We have a lot of time to make up for."

They walked toward the door, and into the future together.

A few of the publications of
THE NAIAD PRESS, INC.
P.O. Box 10543 • Tallahassee, Florida 32302
Phone (904) 539-5965
Toll-Free Order Number: 1-800-533-1973
Mail orders welcome. Please include 15% postage.
Write or call for our free catalog which also features an
incredible selection of lesbian videos.

COSTA BRAVA by Marta Balletbo Coll. 144 pp. Read the book,
see the movie!   ISBN 1-56280-153-8 $11.95

MEETING MAGDALENE & OTHER STORIES by
Marilyn Freeman. 160 pp. Read the book, see the movie!
                                               ISBN 1-56280-170-8   11.95

SECOND FIDDLE by Kate Calloway. 240 pp. P.I. Cassidy James'
second case.   ISBN 1-56280-169-6   11.95

LAUREL by Isabel Miller. 128 pp. By the author of the beloved
Patience and Sarah.   ISBN 1-56280-146-5   10.95

LOVE OR MONEY by Jackie Calhoun. 240 pp. The romance of
real life.   ISBN 1-56280-147-3   10.95

SMOKE AND MIRRORS by Pat Welch. 224 pp. 5th Helen Black
Mystery.   ISBN 1-56280-143-0   10.95

DANCING IN THE DARK edited by Barbara Grier & Christine
Cassidy. 272 pp. Erotic love stories by Naiad Press authors.
                                               ISBN 1-56280-144-9   14.95

TIME AND TIME AGAIN by Catherine Ennis. 176 pp. Passionate
love affair.   ISBN 1-56280-145-7   10.95

PAXTON COURT by Diane Salvatore. 256 pp. Erotic and wickedly
funny contemporary tale about the business of learning to live
together.   ISBN 1-56280-114-7   10.95

INNER CIRCLE by Claire McNab. 208 pp. 8th Carol Ashton
Mystery.   ISBN 1-56280-135-X   10.95

LESBIAN SEX: AN ORAL HISTORY by Susan Johnson.
240 pp. Need we say more?   ISBN 1-56280-142-2   14.95

BABY, IT'S COLD by Jaye Maiman. 256 pp. 5th Robin Miller
Mystery.   ISBN 1-56280-141-4   19.95

WILD THINGS by Karin Kallmaker. 240 pp. By the undisputed
mistress of lesbian romance.   ISBN 1-56280-139-2   10.95

THE GIRL NEXT DOOR by Mindy Kaplan. 208 pp. Just what
you'd expect.   ISBN 1-56280-140-6   10.95

NOW AND THEN by Penny Hayes. 240 pp. Romance on the
westward journey.   ISBN 1-56280-121-X   10.95

HEART ON FIRE by Diana Simmonds. 176 pp. The romantic and
erotic rival of *Curious Wine*.   ISBN 1-56280-152-X   10.95

DEATH AT LAVENDER BAY by Lauren Wright Douglas. 208 pp.
1st Allison O'Neil Mystery.   ISBN 1-56280-085-X   10.95

YES I SAID YES I WILL by Judith McDaniel. 272 pp. Hot
romance by famous author.   ISBN 1-56280-138-4   10.95

FORBIDDEN FIRES by Margaret C. Anderson. Edited by Mathilda
Hills. 176 pp. Famous author's "unpublished" Lesbian romance.
                                           ISBN 1-56280-123-6   21.95

SIDE TRACKS by Teresa Stores. 160 pp. Gender-bending
Lesbians on the road.   ISBN 1-56280-122-8   10.95

HOODED MURDER by Annette Van Dyke. 176 pp. 1st Jessie
Batelle Mystery.   ISBN 1-56280-134-1   10.95

WILDWOOD FLOWERS by Julia Watts. 208 pp. Hilarious and
heart-warming tale of true love.   ISBN 1-56280-127-9   10.95

NEVER SAY NEVER by Linda Hill. 224 pp. Rule #1: Never get involved
with . . .   ISBN 1-56280-126-0   10.95

THE SEARCH by Melanie McAllester. 240 pp. Exciting top cop
Tenny Mendoza case.   ISBN 1-56280-150-3   10.95

THE WISH LIST by Saxon Bennett. 192 pp. Romance through
the years.   ISBN 1-56280-125-2   10.95

FIRST IMPRESSIONS by Kate Calloway. 208 pp. P.I. Cassidy
James' first case.   ISBN 1-56280-133-3   10.95

OUT OF THE NIGHT by Kris Bruyer. 192 pp. Spine-tingling
thriller.   ISBN 1-56280-120-1   10.95

NORTHERN BLUE by Tracey Richardson. 224 pp. Police recruits
Miki & Miranda — passion in the line of fire. ISBN 1-56280-118-X 10.95

LOVE'S HARVEST by Peggy J. Herring. 176 pp. by the author of
Once More With Feeling.   ISBN 1-56280-117-1   10.95

THE COLOR OF WINTER by Lisa Shapiro. 208 pp. Romantic
love beyond your wildest dreams.   ISBN 1-56280-116-3   10.95

FAMILY SECRETS by Laura DeHart Young. 208 pp. Enthralling
romance and suspense.   ISBN 1-56280-119-8   10.95

INLAND PASSAGE by Jane Rule. 288 pp. Tales exploring conven-
tional & unconventional relationships.   ISBN 0-930044-56-8   10.95

DOUBLE BLUFF by Claire McNab. 208 pp. 7th Carol Ashton
Mystery.   ISBN 1-56280-096-5   10.95

BAR GIRLS by Lauran Hoffman. 176 pp. See the movie, read
the book!   ISBN 1-56280-115-5   10.95

THE FIRST TIME EVER edited by Barbara Grier & Christine
Cassidy. 272 pp. Love stories by Naiad Press authors.
                                     ISBN 1-56280-086-8   14.95

MISS PETTIBONE AND MISS McGRAW by Brenda Weathers.
208 pp. A charming ghostly love story.   ISBN 1-56280-151-1   10.95

CHANGES by Jackie Calhoun. 208 pp. Involved romance and
relationships.   ISBN 1-56280-083-3   10.95

FAIR PLAY by Rose Beecham. 256 pp. 3rd Amanda Valentine
Mystery.   ISBN 1-56280-081-7   10.95

PAYBACK by Celia Cohen. 176 pp. A gripping thriller of romance,
revenge and betrayal.   ISBN 1-56280-084-1   10.95

THE BEACH AFFAIR by Barbara Johnson. 224 pp. Sizzling
summer romance/mystery/intrigue.   ISBN 1-56280-090-6   10.95

GETTING THERE by Robbi Sommers. 192 pp. Nobody does it
like Robbi!   ISBN 1-56280-099-X   10.95

FINAL CUT by Lisa Haddock. 208 pp. 2nd Carmen Ramirez
Mystery.   ISBN 1-56280-088-4   10.95

FLASHPOINT by Katherine V. Forrest. 256 pp. A Lesbian
blockbuster!   ISBN 1-56280-079-5   10.95

CLAIRE OF THE MOON by Nicole Conn. Audio Book —Read
by Marianne Hyatt.   ISBN 1-56280-113-9   16.95

FOR LOVE AND FOR LIFE: INTIMATE PORTRAITS OF
LESBIAN COUPLES by Susan Johnson. 224 pp.
                                     ISBN 1-56280-091-4   14.95

DEVOTION by Mindy Kaplan. 192 pp. See the movie — read
the book!   ISBN 1-56280-093-0   10.95

SOMEONE TO WATCH by Jaye Maiman. 272 pp. 4th Robin
Miller Mystery.   ISBN 1-56280-095-7   10.95

GREENER THAN GRASS by Jennifer Fulton. 208 pp. A young
woman — a stranger in her bed.   ISBN 1-56280-092-2   10.95

TRAVELS WITH DIANA HUNTER by Regine Sands. Erotic
lesbian romp. Audio Book (2 cassettes)   ISBN 1-56280-107-4   16.95

CABIN FEVER by Carol Schmidt. 256 pp. Sizzling suspense
and passion.   ISBN 1-56280-089-1   10.95

THERE WILL BE NO GOODBYES by Laura DeHart Young. 192
pp. Romantic love, strength, and friendship.   ISBN 1-56280-103-1   10.95

FAULTLINE by Sheila Ortiz Taylor. 144 pp. Joyous comic
lesbian novel.   ISBN 1-56280-108-2   9.95

OPEN HOUSE by Pat Welch. 176 pp. 4th Helen Black Mystery.
                                     ISBN 1-56280-102-3   10.95

ONCE MORE WITH FEELING by Peggy J. Herring. 240 pp.
Lighthearted, loving romantic adventure.   ISBN 1-56280-089-2   10.95

FOREVER by Evelyn Kennedy. 224 pp. Passionate romance — love
overcoming all obstacles.   ISBN 1-56280-094-9   10.95

WHISPERS by Kris Bruyer. 176 pp. Romantic ghost story
ISBN 1-56280-082-5   10.95

NIGHT SONGS by Penny Mickelbury. 224 pp. 2nd Gianna Maglione
Mystery.   ISBN 1-56280-097-3   10.95

GETTING TO THE POINT by Teresa Stores. 256 pp. Classic
southern Lesbian novel.   ISBN 1-56280-100-7   10.95

PAINTED MOON by Karin Kallmaker. 224 pp. Delicious
Kallmaker romance.   ISBN 1-56280-075-2   10.95

THE MYSTERIOUS NAIAD edited by Katherine V. Forrest &
Barbara Grier. 320 pp. Love stories by Naiad Press authors.
ISBN 1-56280-074-4   14.95

DAUGHTERS OF A CORAL DAWN by Katherine V. Forrest.
240 pp. Tenth Anniversay Edition.   ISBN 1-56280-104-X   10.95

BODY GUARD by Claire McNab. 208 pp. 6th Carol Ashton
Mystery.   ISBN 1-56280-073-6   10.95

CACTUS LOVE by Lee Lynch. 192 pp. Stories by the beloved
storyteller.   ISBN 1-56280-071-X   9.95

SECOND GUESS by Rose Beecham. 216 pp. 2nd Amanda Valentine
Mystery.   ISBN 1-56280-069-8   9.95

A RAGE OF MAIDENS by Lauren Wright Douglas. 240 pp. 6th Caitlin
Reece Mystery.   ISBN 1-56280-068-X   10.95

TRIPLE EXPOSURE by Jackie Calhoun. 224 pp. Romantic drama
involving many characters.   ISBN 1-56280-067-1   10.95

UP, UP AND AWAY by Catherine Ennis. 192 pp. Delightful
romance.   ISBN 1-56280-065-5   9.95

PERSONAL ADS by Robbi Sommers. 176 pp. Sizzling short
stories.   ISBN 1-56280-059-0   10.95

CROSSWORDS by Penny Sumner. 256 pp. 2nd Victoria Cross
Mystery.   ISBN 1-56280-064-7   9.95

SWEET CHERRY WINE by Carol Schmidt. 224 pp. A novel of
suspense.   ISBN 1-56280-063-9   9.95

These are just a few of the many Naiad Press titles — we are the oldest and
largest lesbian/feminist publishing company in the world. We also offer an
enormous selection of lesbian video products. Please request a complete
catalog. We offer personal service; we encourage and welcome direct mail
orders from individuals who have limited access to bookstores carrying our
publications.